Silent Attack

This was a very intricate game, one with high stakes. That's the way it always went whenever men chose to play by the rules of the gun instead of the rules that applied to everyone else.

Clint listened for the next set of approaching footsteps. His muscles waited without so much as a waver until the exact moment when he lunged to strike at the guard.

This time, there was no surprised look on the other man's face: he seemed to be prepared for Clint's attack, even if he didn't know exactly where or when it would come.

Swinging with the Colt in his fist, Clint saw that his target was going to duck before the handle of his own pistol could make contact with the guard's skull. In response, Clint tried to pull his swing downward, but was still unable to deliver any kind of strike before he pounded against the corner of the house.

Clint fully expected that the noise would bring the whole gang on top of him at any second. Until that time, however, he committed himself to bringing down this one man . . .

DON'T MISS THESE
ALL-ACTION WESTERN SERIES
FROM THE BERKLEY PUBLISHING GROUP

THE GUNSMITH by J. R. Roberts
Clint Adams was a legend among lawmen, outlaws, and ladies.
They called him . . . the Gunsmith.

LONGARM by Tabor Evans
The popular long-running series about Deputy U.S. Marshal
Long—his life, his loves, his fight for justice.

SLOCUM by Jake Logan
Today's longest-running action Western. John Slocum rides
a deadly trail of hot blood and cold steel.

BUSHWHACKERS by B. J. Lanagan
An action-packed series by the creators of Longarm! The
rousing adventures of the most brutal gang of cutthroats ever
assembled—Quantrill's Raiders.

DIAMONDBACK by Guy Brewer
Dex Yancey is Diamondback, a Southern gentleman turned
con man when his brother cheats him out of the family for-
tune. Ladies love him. Gamblers hate him. But nobody pulls
one over on Dex . . .

WILDGUN by Jack Hanson
Will Barlow's continuing search for his daughter, kidnapped
by the Blackfeet Indians who slaughtered the rest of his family.

TEXAS TRACKER by Tom Calhoun
Meet J. T. Law: the most relentless, and dangerous, man-
hunter in all Texas. Where sheriffs and posses fail, he's the
best man to bring in the most vicious outlaws—for a price.

THE GUNSMITH

249

DEADLY GAME

J. R. ROBERTS

JOVE BOOKS, NEW YORK

DEADLY GAME

A Jove Book / published by arrangement with
the author

PRINTING HISTORY
Jove edition / September 2002

Copyright © 2002 by Robert J. Randisi.

All rights reserved.
This book, or parts thereof, may not be reproduced in any form
without permission.
For information address: The Berkley Publishing Group,
a division of Penguin Putnam Inc.,
375 Hudson Street, New York, New York 10014.

Visit our website at
www.penguinputnam.com

ISBN: 0-515-13369-8

A JOVE BOOK®
Jove Books are published by The Berkley Publishing Group,
a division of Penguin Putnam Inc.,
375 Hudson Street, New York, New York 10014.
JOVE and the "J" design
are trademarks belonging to Penguin Putnam Inc.

PRINTED IN THE UNITED STATES OF AMERICA

10 9 8 7 6 5 4 3 2 1

ONE

Jeremiah Garver was a simple man. Having long since grown out of the need to prove himself or test his mettle against any and all comers, he was now at the comfortable age of thirty-two where the only thing that mattered was how he felt about his own life. He didn't much care for what others said about him or the way they watched when he crossed the street.

Instead, the only thing that mattered was whether or not he could live with himself or bear to see what looked back at him in the mirror. In a perfect world, that would have been more than enough for him to have a long and happy life. But as he knew only too well, this world was far from perfect.

After all, in a perfect world, nobody tried to put a bullet through your skull when you weren't looking.

The shot cracked through the air like a whip, making a sound that was less of an explosion and more of a snap. That was enough to tell Jeremiah that the gunman wasn't close by, which also told him that he was probably using a rifle. Instinctively, Jeremiah dropped to the ground, tossing the wood he'd been gathering to all sides.

A whispered curse came to his lips, but he kept it back

out of sheer reflex after having been trained by his wife
of fifteen years to watch what he said in front of the children. Even when hot lead burned over him, he still
thought about the hell he would have to pay if he swore
in front of the wrong ears.

Pressing his chest to the packed soil, he made a fist in
the dirt when he thought once again about those ears he'd
been so careful not to sully with foul language. The children! The children were close by and someone was shooting at him and his house.

Jeremiah scrambled over the ground as a second shot
cracked in the distance. He made a note in the back of
his mind as to how long a space there was between the
sound of the shot and the hiss of the bullet cutting through
the air.

Just under a second.

That meant that whoever was doing the shooting was
far enough away for Jeremiah to have some time to tend
to some very important business.

"What's going on, Pa?" The young boy's voice was
still a bit high, but was getting closer to Jeremiah's own
with each passing day.

Jeremiah was already heading toward the house when
he heard his son's voice. Just as he saw the front door
open, he threw himself toward the porch and slapped the
door shut with a quick, flailing hand. "Stay inside, Kyle!"

"But I heard shooting. What's—"

"Just mind what I say, boy. Where's your sister?"

Jeremiah could hear the shuffle of the boy's feet behind
the door, which was quickly followed by the thump of his
little body against the wall and floor. "She's fetching water from the stream," the boy said in a voice that was
more anxious than afraid. "You want me to get her?"

"No," Jeremiah said in a less abrasive tone. "Just stay
down and wait for me to come back."

There was a momentary silence, quickly broken by another shot that took a bite from the door frame just inches over Jeremiah's head. As the sound from the rifle rolled upon the passing wind, Jeremiah crawled away from the porch and toward the side of the house.

"Should I get your gun, Pa?"

As Jeremiah made it around the house, he shouted over his shoulder, "Yes, son. Get my gun and wait for me."

Once he was away from the porch, Jeremiah got his feet beneath him and started running toward the back of his house. He knew every knothole in every piece of timber in that structure, since he'd built it with his own two hands nearly ten years ago. He didn't have to look at the window panes to know that one was slightly less even than the other, just as he didn't have to see the pictures carved along the bottom of the home by the hands of his children to know they were there. In fact, he thought about those carvings as he raced around the house and turned toward the stream running through the edge of his property.

It was his daughter, Sadie, who'd drawn most of those designs. Her brother, Kyle, had been the one to go over them with his pocketknife despite all the trouble he knew he'd be in if he was caught. And even after he'd caught them and given both kids their punishment, Jeremiah kept those carvings right where he'd found them simply because they'd been put there by the hands that he and his wife had created.

Thinking about the children, Jeremiah straightened up and broke into a run. He knew he'd be presenting the shooter with a bigger target, but that didn't matter one bit to him right then. All he could think about was Sadie's little face and how desperately he needed to keep her from being hurt even in the least.

The shots were coming faster now, but he ignored them all. Just as he ran through the line of trees behind his house, he felt a pinch in his left shoulder and felt the warm trickle of blood soaking into his shirt. Jeremiah ignored those things also, devoting every sense at his command to finding his daughter.

"Sadie," he called out. "Sadie, honey, come to Poppa."

Jeremiah stood with his back turned fully toward the directions where the shots had been coming from, hoping that he could shield his little girl when she came running. Before he could worry too much about her safety, his eight-year-old daughter rushed toward him and wrapped her arms tightly around his waist.

"It's all right," Jeremiah said as he swept her up into his arms and ran as fast as he could through the trees. "Did you get hurt?"

"No, Poppa. But I was real scared."

"I know, sweetie. But don't worry too much . . ." He stopped himself before saying anything else the instant he caught the hint of movement coming from somewhere in front of him and toward the stream. Knowing better than to stop and look too long for the source of the movement, Jeremiah held onto his girl a little tighter and turned to run directly for the house.

All thoughts of his own safety were put aside. When he'd first gotten hold of his daughter, Jeremiah's impulse had been to take a roundabout path back to the house in the hopes that they would draw less fire that way. But now that he was fairly certain there were more gunmen than just the one with the rifle, he could only hope to get his children tucked safely away before having to face his attackers.

He braced himself for the next round of gunfire the moment he was clear of the trees. Although he knew the rifleman probably didn't have a clear shot, Jeremiah expected the figure behind him to open fire even though he could hear nothing coming from that direction. But much like those carvings on the side of his house he couldn't see, just because he couldn't hear that other figure didn't mean it was no longer there.

Jeremiah's heart was racing in his chest. It seemed to take a week of running before he finally made it to his back porch and all but kicked the door off its hinges. "Here you go," he said while gently setting his little girl onto the floor. "Now find a good place to hide and don't come out until I say it's all right. Understand me?"

". . . Yes, Poppa," the girl replied in a meek little voice.

TWO

Satisfied with the sight of his girl scampering off to bury herself in whatever little space she'd discovered, Jeremiah turned around just in time to see a lean figure step out of the trees and walk toward the house. The sound of snapping branches and leaves being crushed underfoot was enough to let him know that the rifleman was making his way down from his perch as well.

It was at that moment that Jeremiah heard the footsteps rushing up behind him from inside the house.

Jeremiah spun around with his fists balled up before he had a chance to push back his fighting instincts. He found himself staring down into the wide, surprised eyes of his son.

"Here you go, Pa," the boy said while hefting a double-rig gun belt in both hands.

Jeremiah nodded, took the belt, and buckled it around his waist. "Good job, Kyle. Now get yourself hid and watch after your sister."

The thirteen-year-old boy was at the age where defying his father had become a daily occurrence. But this time, the fear he was trying so hard to fight back was too much for him to overcome with grace. The color in his face had drained away and his hands were trembling even after the load he'd been carrying had been taken away.

Without another word, Kyle turned and darted back into the house's other room. Jeremiah prayed for both children's safety as he shut the back door and turned to face whoever was coming, wearing the look of a feral wolf protecting its young.

"What the hell do you want?" Jeremiah said to the figure that was now less than twenty feet away.

The figure was narrow in the shoulders and wore a battered leather jacket over a plain white shirt. He moved with the easy step of an experienced hunter, confident that he would have no problem sinking his teeth into his prey.

Coming to a stop, the figure locked eyes with Jeremiah. The revolver in his fist was held low, but aimed directly at Jeremiah's chest.

Jeremiah could feel his guns at his sides. But when his fingertips so much as brushed along the tops of the weapons, he saw the man in front of him tense slightly and shake his head.

"I wouldn't do anything stupid," the figure said. "Not when you've got those little ones of yours about."

Jeremiah's first impulse was to draw his gun and put a bullet right through the other man's smirking face. But he was too experienced in such matters to be taken in by such a simple play on his emotions. He'd seen too many men like this one to be manipulated by him so easily.

Sensing that his words were having their intended effect, the figure narrowed his eyes and glared at Jeremiah. Leaning slightly forward, he let out a slow, hissing breath and said, "Go ahead and pull that heat. I hate to see a man wear two guns without enough guts to even draw one of 'em when push comes to shove."

"My question still stands," Jeremiah said in a measured tone. "What are you doing here?"

"I think you know the answer to that without having to ask."

The picture was getting clearer in Jeremiah's mind. Even so, he hoped beyond hope that he was wrong. Even with what had happened so far, anything would be better than what he was thinking. "Who are you?"

Before he could reply, the figure cocked his head to one side as the set of footsteps that had been drawing closer could once again be heard. He took a step back without taking his eyes away from Jeremiah, nodding slowly as though he was about to see the show he'd been waiting for all afternoon.

Jeremiah recognized a lap dog when he saw one. And as much as he wanted to vent some of his anger on the man who he could see at the moment, he knew well enough that the figure before him was taking orders from the man who was just about to step into view. So rather than jump before the time was right, he stood by and waited for the rifleman to show himself, hoping that his children were taking advantage of every second he was buying them.

The footsteps were steady and light. Obviously, the man taking them was no longer in any hurry since he'd surely heard the conversation between Jeremiah and the other figure. As soon as the footsteps stopped, the wind seemed to die down, almost as though the world around Jeremiah's house had chosen that moment to hold its breath.

Standing a few inches below six feet in height, the newest arrival held himself as though he towered over everyone and everything he could see. His frame was thin and wiry, moving with a fluid grace beneath a long, tan riding coat. He held a Spencer rifle over his shoulder, but soon leveled the weapon at Jeremiah more as a statement than a threat.

The moment he saw the rifleman's face, Jeremiah knew

that his worst fears had been realized. This was the face that he'd spent the last several years trying to forget, but could never manage to fully drag from the back of his mind. This was the last face he would ever want to see this close to his own home.

"Jeremiah Garver," the rifleman said. "You're a hard man to find."

Trying not to show any of the fears that played through his mind like a waking nightmare, Jeremiah swallowed hard and said, "I do my best. Where's the rest of your men, Brody?"

"What makes you think I need more than this one here?"

"Because you never only work with one other man. I spent too many years riding with you not to know something like that."

Looking from Jeremiah to the other figure, Brody stepped a bit closer and took more careful aim with the Spencer. "Marcus is better than the type that used to ride with us in the old days. Hell, he was good enough to get the drop on you, wasn't he?"

"Maybe. But I had other things to do besides put him down."

"That's right," Brody said. "You did. That little girl of yours. What's her name? Sadie? And your son, Kyle. You had to tuck them away before coming out to meet with your old friends."

"Old friends don't shoot at you before saying hello," Jeremiah snapped. "Now state your business and get the hell off my land."

Any trace of civility, no matter how false, vanished from Brody's face. With a quick twitch of his left hand, he levered a fresh round into the Spencer. "You're right about one thing. I do have others with me. And they'll be more than happy to blow that cabin of yours into splinters unless you watch that smart-ass mouth."

Jeremiah's face became hard as stone. After the initial shock of seeing the familiar face had worked through his system, he was able to steel himself against the wild thumping of his heart and all the horrific images that filled his imagination when Brody mentioned his children. Slowly easing his hands away from his guns, Jeremiah let his arms drop to his sides and nodded slowly. "All right, Brody. No need to make threats like that. You caught me off my guard, that's all."

Not relaxing one bit, Brody spoke with his jaw clenched. Each word came through his teeth like venom from the mouth of a rattlesnake. "It ain't no threat. I say the word, and your young ones become ghosts just like their momma. And you won't be joining them before taking a few years to mourn them while locked up in a cage with every bone in your body broke."

The fortitude that Jeremiah had managed to build up quickly melted away. "You speak one more word about my Jenny and I'll kill you."

Once he saw that he'd broken through the other man's stony facade, Brody eased back a step, grinning in satisfaction. "Glad to see you've still got the fire in you. I was thinking family life might've made you soft." Lifting his head, he turned in a slow circle while speaking to the land around him. "Come on down, boys. Let's make ourselves at home."

With that, no fewer than eight other figures appeared on the ridge and trees surrounding the house. Jeremiah felt the bottom drop from his stomach, knowing that this nightmare had just begun.

THREE

Having just ridden through Oklahoma after a few unscheduled stops, Clint Adams was glad to be in the middle of some green lands for a change. At least, they were probably really green at another time of year. At the moment, most of the trees were shedding their leaves to create a thick bed of crunching foliage beneath Eclipse's feet. It was the middle of autumn and wouldn't get half as cold as the country farther north, but it was obvious by the chill in the air that summer was most definitely gone.

Clint had no particular destination in mind, other than the simple desire to ride wherever his desires took him. For the last few days, those desires had taken him east, over the Arkansas border, and into the mountains that covered that lush southern state. The trails weren't easy, but they were surrounded with beautiful scenery and rich, fragrant air.

Even at this time of year, the air still managed to have a current of warmth beneath the chill. He knew he wouldn't be thinking about that chill so fondly once night fell and he was left to sleep beneath the stars, but for the moment Clint was enjoying it just fine. Besides, he knew there was a town less than a few hours away.

Knowing that Eclipse could be trusted to stay on course, Clint allowed his eyes to wander away from the trail and take in the breathtaking sights all around him. The mountains loomed in the distance. The sky was filled with clouds that looked like white smudges upon a blue canvas. And amid it all, the trees were everywhere, stretching in every direction to wrap around him like a giant shawl.

Clint took a deep breath of fragrant air and closed his eyes for no more than a second before snapping them open. "Did you hear that?" he said to himself.

Eclipse recognized the sound of his master immediately. The Darley Arabian's ears twitched on top of his head and his head bobbed up and down as if in response to Clint's question.

But Clint was too distracted to pay attention to the stallion. The sound he'd just heard still echoed vaguely in the distance, but it might as well have been blaring in his thoughts. He'd heard that sound way too many times for it to go by unnoticed. And no matter how much he tried to put it out of his mind, there simply was no mistaking the sound of gunfire.

Clint pulled back on the reins just enough to bring Eclipse to a stop. His eyes darted back and forth as he did his best to keep absolutely quiet. He even held his breath for a few seconds while waiting to see if that distinctive cracking sound would come back.

He didn't have to wait long before another shot was fired. Clint knew well enough that it could have been locals shooting their supper in the hills around him, but too many years of wandering into the strangest of situations made him doubt that he could come upon something as simple as a hunting party.

Snapping the reins, Clint held on as Eclipse broke into a run. He steered the Darley Arabian stallion toward the shots that continued to filter in from the trail ahead. The more he rode, the more Clint thought he wouldn't find anything besides a couple of kids shooting squirrels. But then again, it was always best to announce your presence before unintentionally riding through someone else's line of fire.

Clint heard another shot just as he caught sight of a group of horses standing in a grassy clearing just to the side of the trail. A quick count turned up eleven of the animals and by the looks of them, they didn't belong to simple local hunters. After bringing Eclipse to a stop, Clint decided to climb down from the saddle and get a closer look for himself.

He was careful not to step on anything that would make too much noise as he approached the horses. All the while, he kept his ears and eyes open for the first hint of anyone else nearby that stood on only two legs.

Sure enough, Clint's ears were rewarded by the snap of a twig no more than ten feet to his left. He reflexively ducked into a stand of bushes nearby, just as a man holding a shotgun walked by. Clint knew better than to trust the sparse bushes he'd chosen as cover and braced himself to be inevitably discovered.

The man with the shotgun was moving slow enough to give Clint a chance to look him over. Although he held the gun at the ready, he didn't seem too anxious to use it. It wasn't so much that he was afraid, but cautious and unwilling to pull the trigger without probable cause.

Any doubt in Clint's mind regarding the question of the man being a hunter was instantly put to rest when he saw that the shotgun's barrel had been sawed off. The only thing a man hunted with a sawed-off shotgun was another man.

The shotgunner took another couple of steps. His eyes swept over the trail and focused immediately upon Eclipse. He thumbed back both hammers of his weapon and held it at the ready.

"Hello there," Clint said, being careful not to startle the shotgunner too much.

The shotgunner planted his feet and took aim. "Get out of there," he snarled. "What're you doin' hidin' in them bushes?"

"I wasn't hiding, exactly," Clint said in a slightly embarrassed voice. "I was . . . umm . . . answering the call of nature, you might say."

Hearing that, the shotgunner grinned slightly and relaxed his posture. The weapon in his hands, however, did not waver so much as an inch from where he'd aimed it. "Well, pull up your britches, get on your horse, and ride away. Be quick about it."

Clint was no stage actor, but he put on his best meek expression and shuffled out of the bushes. After having become strangely accustomed to being at gunpoint, it was kind of refreshing to get out of one of those situations without having to draw his own weapon in kind.

On his way toward Eclipse, Clint took a closer look at the horses that were tied up in the nearby clearing. As he suspected, the saddles were each outfitted with rifle holsters and lacked any trapping gear or other supplies needed for hunting. That, along with the guard that was eyeing him suspiciously, was more than enough to prove Clint's theory that the men who'd ridden in on those horses were after something bigger than small game.

FOUR

Clint could feel the shotgunner's eyes boring through him like a pair of drills, slowly turning deeper into him the longer he took in his walk back to Eclipse. But he could also hear something else in the distance that made him decide to test the guard's limits rather than simply hurry out of his sights.

"You had your squat in the bushes," the guard said with growing impatience. "Now get your ass out of here before I put my boot in it."

Forcing back his reflexive response for those kind of words, Clint managed to appear intimidated by the other man and shrugged apologetically. Just as he was going to say something to further the ruse, he heard that sound in the distance one more time.

Before, he hadn't been too sure. But now that he knew what to listen for, he was all but certain that there was somebody screaming farther up the trail. It wasn't just a panicked cry, either, but someone shouting a name. Whoever it was, they sounded afraid for their life.

"Sadie!" the voice had said. There was more, but at this distance, Clint couldn't quite make it out.

He was halfway to Eclipse when Clint heard that name

being called out. Certain that there was something bad
going on, he stopped and turned around to face the shotgunner head-on. "What was that?" he asked.

The shotgunner didn't pretend to be deaf to the distant
shouting. In fact, he didn't even sound surprised to hear
it. "That's none of your concern, mister. So take my ad-
vice: get on that horse and ride away before it's too late."

Clint took another step forward. Something deep inside
his gut told him that whoever was doing the screaming
wasn't doing so just to hear the sound of their own voice.
And whoever this Sadie turned out to be was probably in
even greater danger.

Motioning toward the other horses, Clint said, "The rest
of your friends are chasing someone down. And since I
don't see any badge on your chest, I've got to assume that
you all are chasing him for no good reason."

The shotgunner's face darkened with aggression. His
fists tightened around his weapon and he planted his feet
as though bracing for the recoil when he pulled the trigger. Despite all of that, he still didn't fire. And it was that
simple fact that told Clint all he needed to know.

This one was dangerous, but he wasn't sure of himself.

"I can see why they left you behind to watch the animals," Clint said while taking a cautious step forward.

"Not another move," the shotgunner warned through
tight lips. "I swear, I'll put you down."

Clint measured the guard carefully. Using all his years
of experience as well as a set of finely honed instincts, he
summed up the shotgunner in the space of a second or
two. "You ever use that shotgun? Ever fire it at someone
like this?"

The guard started to say something, but all he could
get out was a nervous sputter.

"Because I don't think you have," Clint continued as
he took another step. "You're too jittery. You thought you

had the sand for this kind of work, but you soon found out differently. You're no killer."

Clint was less than five feet away now. That was close enough to make the shotgunner lift his weapon up and press it to his shoulder. His eyes were twitching as he churned up the strength to pull back on that trigger.

Moving as though he was going to take a step back, Clint only began the step before lunging forward like a striking cobra. The initial fake was enough to put the shotgunner at ease for a split second, which was all Clint needed to reach out and grab hold of the shotgun's barrel, twisting it hard enough to snap the guard's finger before it tightened around the trigger.

The bone made a wet, cracking sound as it broke, which was Clint's cue to pull the gun sideways and completely out of the other man's grasp. Even through the pain etched across his features, the guard looked even more stunned at the fact that he was suddenly left with nothing but a broken finger where his shotgun used to be.

When Clint's body came to a stop, he was standing with his shoulders squared and the shotgun leveled at its former owner. "Now let's try this again," he said patiently. "Where's the owners of those horses and what are they up to?"

Wincing as a wave of pain shot up from his hand and all the way through his arm, the guard took in a sharp breath. He was actually trying to ball up his fists and come after Clint, but once he was reminded about his broken bone, he decided to abandon the idea.

"It don't matter what you do to me," the guard said. "You ain't got a prayer against all of 'em once they know you're fixin' to take them on."

Clint nodded. "Fine. So are you going to answer my questions or should I pick something else to break?"

Now the guard started to smile. "They're down the road a stretch. If you're stupid enough to try anything with

Brody, then you deserve whatever happens to you."

"How many are there?"

"Counting me . . . eleven."

"And what are they shooting at? Or should I say . . . *who* are they shooting at?"

"Just some old-timer Brody knew a while back. Someone else who didn't know when to back off and count their blessings while they was still healthy."

"Yeah," Clint said. "I guess I've been counted in that group more than once myself. Can I trust you to stay put and keep your mouth shut?"

A glint of hope shone in the guard's eyes, followed by a poorly disguised look of treacherousness. "Sure! I mean, what am I going to do with a broken hand, right? I know when to—"

"On second thought, you just talked me out of it," Clint interrupted. Although the notion of trusting the guard had never really entered his mind, it was amusing to see the other man's mind race with the possibilities of stabbing him in the back. A little on the mean side, but amusing nonetheless.

After taking a few minutes to hog-tie the guard and gag him with his own bandanna, Clint tossed the shotgun into the bushes and made his way down the trail.

FIVE

Jeremiah had never before felt so uncomfortable inside his own little house. It always seemed so cozy when his family was inside its walls. Even on the few occasions when they'd entertained company, the place felt warm and inviting. Now, with Brody's men filling up the main room as well as the bedrooms and a few more patrolling the outside, the house felt less like a home and more like a prison.

Brody was sitting at the head of the family's little dining table, lounging in a chair with his feet kicked up on the tabletop. He worked a toothpick between his front teeth, casually grooming himself as though he'd just polished off a fine meal. All around him, his men made themselves comfortable without any regard to Jeremiah's belongings or property. In fact, they'd gone out of their way to dump the contents of cabinets, chests, and pantries onto the floor while joking to each other about the mess they'd made.

Jeremiah watched all of this feeling hopeless and powerless. Every time a plate shattered or a window was knocked out, he flinched and felt his muscles tense. Any other time and he would have worked his way through

these men one at a time. The only thing holding him back
was the fact that none of the invaders had found either of
his children yet.

That fact alone was enough to spark the tiniest bit of
hope at the center of his soul. He might have been a little
more hopeful if his guns hadn't been taken from him.

"So where are they?" Brody asked, as though reading
Jeremiah's thoughts.

Knowing better than to try and bluff the leader of the
invaders, Jeremiah kept staring straight ahead and acted
as though he hadn't even heard the question.

Brody's fist came smashing down on the table, causing
everyone inside the house to flinch. "Don't even pretend
with me, Jeremiah. You never was no good at it and you
ain't any better now. Where are them little bastards you
call children?"

Jeremiah maintained his silence, although he did turn
slowly to look Brody in the face. The look he gave the
other man was powerful enough to ignite dry kindling.
The hatred in his eyes burned through like sunlight focused through a magnifying glass.

"Might as well tell me now while I'm still feeling char-
itable," Brody said, his eyes bearing Jeremiah's hatred
without faltering. "Because once my men start getting fed
up with looking, they're liable to become awful cranky."

With that, some of the men standing around the table
laughed under their breaths. As far as Jeremiah could tell,
only a few of the others were looking in the other rooms
for the children. And he could only tell that by the stomp-
ing of their feet and the occasional item being smashed
upon the floor.

Jeremiah knew that if either of the children had been
found, the gunmen would have been sure to let him know
about it. Also, he was fairly certain that if they hadn't
been found by now, both Kyle and Sadie had probably

gotten away. He could only hope they knew enough to stay put wherever they were.

"You should know me well enough to know that I wouldn't hand over my kids to you any sooner than I'd chew my own leg off," Jeremiah said plainly. "So while your men keep looking, why don't you just say whatever it is you came here to say."

After glancing around to his men and looking in on the progress of those who were still turning the bedrooms upside down, Brody shrugged and said, "All right. I guess we'll know as soon as those kids turn up when they start screamin'." He waited a few seconds for the threat to sink in, studying Jeremiah's face carefully. All he found was the familiar visage that might as well have been carved from the side of a mountain. "I need your help on a job I've lined up."

Jeremiah couldn't help but laugh. At first, the smile that crept across his face felt strange. It was an uncomfortable reflex rather than anything coming from any sense of joy. The more he thought about what he'd just heard, the funnier it seemed, until finally he was laughing hard enough for his shoulders to shake and his belly to jump up and down beneath his shirt.

After a while, tears rolled down his face. Jeremiah reached up to wipe them away, his eyes glancing around at all the other men without truly seeing any of them. "You . . . need my help?" he asked between chuckles. "You came all this way, tracked me down, shot at me, and threatened my children all because you need my help?"

Although Brody seemed somewhat amused by the other man's response, he didn't seem to share any of Jeremiah's levity. "That's right. I'm glad to see you find that so damn amusing."

"If this is the way you ask for help, I'd hate to see what you do when you're looking for a wife." Jeremiah paused as he was shaken by another wave of laughter. "How do you pay your respects to family? Ride by and take shots at their windows?"

Brody's smile quickly faded. "You should know how I pay respects to my family," he said in a harsh tone. "You were there when I buried my brother. If it wasn't for you, he'd still be alive." The gunman pressed his hands upon the table and put his weight on them as he leaned forward to push his face closer to Jeremiah's. "And you should know that I'm real tempted to bury your family just like you buried mine. Since your kin and wife are already feeding the worms, that just leaves your kids."

Suddenly, Jeremiah's face grew dark. All that was left of the nervous laughter was its echo floating around the ceiling he'd built. He took a deep breath and tried not to think about the extraordinary danger his children were in. After having known Brody for almost twenty years, he knew what the man was capable of and killing children was well within his abilities.

"What's the job?" Jeremiah asked.

Brody nodded. Steepling his fingers, he leaned back and resumed his self-important posture at the head of the table. "Ah yes. I knew you wouldn't have to wait for that little girl to start crying before you were ready to talk business. Some of the boys had a bet that you'd have to see their blood before you'd—"

"Shut your damn mouth," Jeremiah snapped. Although there was some defiance in his voice, the look in his eyes was that of a defeated man. "Just call your men in and let my children go. I'll do whatever you want."

SIX

Fully confident in his ability to tie a strong knot, Clint moved ahead on the trail and allowed himself to forget about the guard he'd left behind. Even in the autumn, the Arkansas foliage was dense and cumbersome. Leaves covered the trail like a thick carpet, making it all but impossible to track anything smaller than a caravan.

Fortunately, the people ahead didn't seem too concerned with keeping quiet. Gunshots and shouting voices could be heard at regular intervals, acting as a beacon to Clint as he worked his way toward the source of all the commotion.

Before too long, the gunshots died down, giving way to lowered voices and more footsteps rustling through the dry, dead leaves. With the brush acting as a filter for the noise in the area, it seemed as though the sounds were always just out of Clint's reach. One moment, it seemed as though he was right on top of them and the next, he felt a mile away. Clint was just about to start running when he heard something he knew had to be less than five feet away from him.

The sound wasn't much, but it was enough to alert his senses, which were already straining to catch anything that seemed remotely out of place. Not much more than a rustling in the leaves, the noise wouldn't have caught his attention if not for the whispered "shhh" that quickly followed it.

Clint froze and took a moment to scan his surroundings. The first time, his eyes passed right over them. But on his next glance over the bushes next to the trail, he caught sight of two figures huddled together, keeping almost as still as the rocks behind them.

Keeping his hand on the grip of his modified Colt, Clint took a few more steps in the same direction he'd been going and then worked his way over the ridge that led down to the source of the earlier gunshots.

Kyle watched the strange man stop and move for his pistol. The young boy swore the man looked directly at the spot where he and his sister were hiding, but then the stranger looked away and headed off in another direction.

Turning to his sister, who was crouched down beside him with her arms wrapped around his waist and her face buried in his shirt, Kyle looked down at her and swatted her on the side of her head. "You almost got us caught, Sadie."

"I'm sorry," the little girl replied, a waver developing in her voice that would soon turn into a full sob. "I didn't mean to."

Kyle put his hand on her shoulder and patted her consolingly. "I know," he whispered. "But we just gotta keep quiet is all. Pa told us to stay hid until he comes for us."

"When will Poppa come? I'm scared."

"I know. Me too."

Trying not to think about what happened to his father or what kind of trouble they all might be in, Kyle scooted forward a little closer to the edge of the bushes and peered in between a few bare branches. As far as he could tell, there wasn't anyone else coming. In fact, he couldn't even hear what that other man with the shotgun was doing back by all the horses.

Kyle knew these parts like the back of his small hand. He and his sister played hide-and-seek here all the time. They'd even run off this way when they wanted to dodge a whipping from their father whenever he took a switch off one of the trees.

Thinking about his pa, even on those rare times when he handed out whippings, Kyle felt hot tears burning the corners of his eyes. He wiped them away quickly, tightening his lips in a grimace of concentration so that his sister wouldn't see him cry. That would only make things worse, he knew. And the only thing worse than Sadie crying right then was . . .

Suddenly, Kyle heard something from the direction of the house.

Like a rabbit caught in the glow of a passing lantern, Kyle froze. He didn't move a muscle in the awkward squatting position he was in, keeping his balance the way that only the young and limber could.

He didn't move his arms.

He didn't even breathe.

The only part of him that did move was his eyes, which darted to and fro in a desperate attempt to get a look at whatever it was that had made the noise he'd just heard.

After a few seconds, Kyle didn't catch so much as a hint of what had made the noise. Before too long, he was starting to doubt if there had been a noise at all. He knew more than anybody that the wind could make a different sound every day. Most of the ghosts he'd been afraid of when he was Sadie's age were just tricks of the wind. That's what Pa had called them, anyway.

Tricks of the wind and nothing to be scared of.

Taking some reassurance from that, Kyle let out the breath he'd been holding and allowed himself to relax. He didn't want to leave Sadie's side for too much longer, so he shuffled around and came face-to-face with that strange man he'd just seen a minute or so ago.

Kyle's first reaction was to scream.

The stranger must've known this because he reached out with both hands and clamped one over Kyle's mouth, placing the other on the back of his head. Kyle felt his screams get soaked up by the stranger's hand. When he tried to struggle, the boy found that he couldn't pull his head free from where he was being held like a bug between the other man's palms.

Just when Kyle was about to lash out with his feet and balled-up fists, he felt the pressure around his skull loosen up a bit. When he opened his eyes, the boy found himself looking directly into the stranger's face.

Unlike the other men who'd ridden up to his house, this one didn't seem so mean. He let go of the back of Kyle's head and put a finger to his lips.

"Shhh," Clint whispered. "I don't want to hurt you. Don't make a sound or those other men will know where we are and they'll come for us."

SEVEN

Kyle didn't know what to make of this man, but he did know that if he screamed, he'd be in even bigger trouble. He'd heard the scuffle between this man and the one with the shotgun, but wasn't quite sure how it had turned out. There were no gunshots and the spot where it had happened was just a little too far away for Kyle to see.

But there was something about this other man. Something that made Kyle think it just might be all right to do what he said. After all, he figured that if he and Sadie could get away from all the others, they could get away from this one if things went too bad.

When the stranger took his hand away, Kyle held back his scream and nodded slowly that he would do what the man asked. Almost immediately, the boy saw the fancy gun in the stranger's holster.

Clint could tell that this boy was scared. But even with fear trembling just beneath the kid's surface, the boy managed to hold himself together.

"Is there anyone else around here?" Clint asked.

When the boy answered, he stopped himself for a second as though he thought that saying anything would break his promise to keep silent. But after thinking it over for another moment or so, he squinted his eyes and studied Clint carefully. "No," he said in a wavering tone. "It's just me. I got away."

Clint could tell the boy was lying. Kyle's deception was written all over his face like a tribal tattoo. It was in the twitch of his eye and the slight upward turn at the corner of his mouth. But just to keep the kid comfortable, Clint went along with it all the same. "Then you're awful brave. I don't want to attract the attention of whoever was doing the shooting so I need you to come with me so we can get somewhere safe."

Kyle took a few steps with Clint, started to look over his shoulder and then stopped himself at the last minute.

Pretending to ignore what the boy was doing, Clint kept himself crouched low and walking toward the ridge overlooking the area where he'd heard the shooting. "Good thing you're alone," he said quietly. "If anyone else was left behind, they'd be caught for sure once we leave them. If we're going to get away clean, we need to stick tog—"

That was more than Kyle could handle. His features twisted beneath the weight of the situation and he finally cracked. "I . . . I'm not by myself," he stammered.

Just then, Clint could hear a rustling in the brush nearby. Although he couldn't make out any details through the tangle of branches, he could see a small figure huddled down in a tight leapfrog position. The figure was too big to be an animal and too small to be an adult. Clint kept the figure in the corner of his eye and pretended not to see it.

"You're not by yourself?" Clint asked with mock surprise.

Kyle shook his head. "My sister's with me. We both got out together." He motioned toward the small figure in the bushes and held his arms open to receive the little girl. "Her name's Sadie."

Clint watched the small girl crawl out from her hiding spot. Like her brother, every inch of her hands and face were covered with a layer of dirt. Small scratches crossed one cheek, none of them deep enough to be of much concern.

Waiting until the brother and sister were huddled together, Clint held out his hand and shook first Kyle's hand and then Sadie's little fist. "My name's Clint. Can you tell me what happened?"

Sadie's light blue eyes were wide and frightened. She looked up at her brother with complete trust. It was still too early for her to look at Clint head-on, but she kept trying every few seconds anyway.

Keeping one arm wrapped tightly around his sister, Kyle focused his eyes on Clint, doing his best to summon up as much ferocity as his youthful soul could muster. "They came for my pa. They said they wanted to get us too, but Pa told us to run and hide."

"You did a good job of that," Clint said, thinking about the guard not too far back along the trail who hadn't even known these kids were here. "Do you know who those men are?"

Kyle shook his head solemnly.

"Did your father know who they were?"

Kyle's eyes rolled upward and then to either side as though he was looking for the answer in the air around Clint's face. Finally, he shrugged with both shoulders. "I guess I don't know."

Clint looked toward the edge of the ridge that led down toward the end of the trail. Keeping his hand on the boy's shoulder so he could make sure Kyle didn't get too far away, he shuffled along the side of the trail until he could look down onto the other side of the ridge. "Do you know how many there were?" he asked, not really expecting much of an answer.

"Ten," Kyle replied almost instantly.

Since Clint had just been trying to keep the kids thinking about something besides running away, he'd actually been talking more to himself than them. Turning to look at the boy, he asked, "Are you sure? Did you see them all?"

Kyle nodded vigorously, a look of annoyance crossing his face. "Yeah, I saw them. I know how to count."

"So do I," Sadie chimed in proudly.

When Clint looked down at the girl, he found her staring straight back at him. She didn't turn away, but she still seemed a little afraid when he kept her in his sight. Rather than frighten her, Clint smiled and patted her head. It seemed strange at the time, but somehow it also felt like a natural thing to do.

"Well, if I've got both of your words on it, I guess that's how many there are."

Looking down on the other side of the ridge, Clint immediately lost the smile he'd been wearing for the children's sake. He counted four men walking the perimeter of a small house situated amid a couple of well-tended gardens and a few pens used to keep small animals along with a few horses. Behind the house was a smaller shed just big enough to contain a workbench and tools or possibly a small carriage.

All in all, the setup looked fairly comfortable . . . as long as the guards walking around the place weren't figured into the equation.

EIGHT

He waited another couple of seconds, but still only picked out the same four men he'd spotted originally. If the kids and the guard could be taken for their word, and Clint couldn't sense anything but certainty in their count, then that meant there were still six other men left unaccounted for, either inside the house or patrolling farther away and out of Clint's sight.

There was a spyglass in his saddlebags that would help Clint immensely in trying to spot the remaining men. But going back to fetch it would mean either taking the kids with him or leaving them where they were. Neither of those options was too appealing and besides that, whoever was inside that house with the gunmen was undoubtedly in a precarious situation. Every moment that went by might just bring the kids' father closer to a bad end.

"All right," Clint said after making his decision. "I'm going to head down there and see what's going on."

Sadie's first reaction was to shake her head hard enough to send her light blond hair into a flurry all around her face. "No," she whispered. "Don't go. They'll hurt you just like they hurt Poppa."

Clint looked into the little girl's face and spoke with

complete sincerity. "You can stay here and keep hiding because you're so good at that. You and your brother will be safe while I go and see what I can do to help your father."

She still seemed scared, but wasn't about to say anything about it.

Turning to Kyle, Clint asked, "Is there anything you can tell me that might help? Any peculiar things about them? Did they mention any names?"

Kyle thought about it hard. "I heard one of them call another one Brody. Does that help?"

"Yeah," Clint said, even though it didn't. "You both did real good. Now stay here and stay hidden. Watch for me or your father to come and get you."

"Mister?" came Sadie's voice.

Clint was just about to start moving when he heard her, so he stopped and turned to face the little girl. "What is it?"

"Are you really going to help my poppa?"

"I'll try. I certainly will try."

Making sure to keep his head low, Clint moved away from the bushes and put some distance between himself and where the children were still standing. If any of the guards he could or couldn't see should happen to spot him, he wanted to be certain that they at least didn't get a look at the kids as well. Clint shuffled as quickly as he could in the sparse cover that was available to him until he made it a comfortable distance away from Kyle and Sadie.

Looking back, Clint stopped for a moment to check if the kids had done what they were supposed to or not. His heart skipped a beat when he thought both of them had taken off on their own, since they were nowhere to be seen. But once Clint looked a little harder, he could make out their vague outlines in the bushes and then he could spot both of their faces staring back at him from masterfully chosen hiding spots.

If he hadn't known exactly what to look for and where, even Clint might have passed them over. He took some comfort from the fact that they seemed more than capable of staying out of harm's way . . . at least for the time being.

The hill was steep at first, sloping down from the upper part of the ridge where the horses were tethered and gradually easing into a gentler decline that led straight to the small, modest homestead. There weren't a whole lot of places for a grown man to hide, especially once he broke free from the surrounding bushes. The only reason Clint made it as far as he did without attracting immediate attention was that he managed to time his descent at a point when the guards were farthest away from him as they slowly walked around the main house.

Clint could feel the guard's eyes on him as the other man walked around the house, idly scanning the surrounding area for whatever it was he'd been commanded to look for. Just when Clint was certain he was about to be spotted, the guard stopped and glanced up directly at him.

The second that followed seemed to take an hour to pass.

Although he couldn't make out all the details on the guard's face from the distance he was away from the other man, Clint would have bet everything he had that the man next to the house was staring right into his eyes. The figure down at the bottom of the ridge kept perfectly still, craning his neck as though he was trying to get a better look at something that had caught his interest.

Clint found he was holding his breath until finally the guard moved again . . . and kept right on moving as he walked around the corner of the house and disappeared. For a second, Clint was stunned. He hadn't been trying to get caught, but he knew better than to think he could get too far before he was spotted.

Then again, he'd long ago trained himself to expect the unexpected. Some things, however, were simply more unexpected than others.

Taking advantage of his good luck and the lazy eye of a bored guard, Clint made his way farther down the ridge until he was close enough to make out a few shapes moving back and forth in a constant pacing pattern through the house's windows.

Clint was almost at the bottom of the incline when he heard another set of footsteps coming around from the side of the house. This time, he knew better than to sit still and take his chances yet again. Instead, he drew his Colt and rushed as fast as he could toward the house. Luckily, the ground was mostly packed soil and didn't make too much noise as he stepped quickly over it.

His back didn't get to touch the house's wall before Clint saw the first hint of movement coming from around the small building. He let the guard step into view and turn the corner before raising the Colt just over his head and moving forward.

The guard's eyes widened as he took in the sight of Clint coming at him and was just about to give a warning to his partners before his words were cut off. Clint brought his hand down as though he was cracking a whip, striking the guard on the temple with the butt of his gun.

A surprised croak gurgled up from the guard's throat as Clint's Colt put a neat dent in the side of his head. His body tried reflexively to defend itself, but before it could do much of anything, the impact of the blow dropped him forward and into Clint's waiting arms.

One down, Clint thought. Nine to go.

NINE

Every one of Brody's men crowded around Jeremiah like buzzards trying to get the biggest scrap of dead meat for themselves. They eyed him as though his death sentence had already been passed down, glancing occasionally to their boss for the word to indulge their bloody desires.

Brody could feel his men's anxiousness and purposely let it build since he knew Jeremiah could feel it too. "So, are you ready to listen to the deal I came all this way to offer you?"

"Do I have a choice?"

Brody allowed himself to grin slightly and got to his feet. "Sure," he said smugly. "You can always try to run away from me again like you did last time. I've got to hand it to you. It did take me quite a while to track you down. I never figured you for the homestead type."

"Just cut through the bullshit and say what you came to say," Jeremiah snarled. "What's the job?"

Hearing the contempt in Jeremiah's tone, one of Brody's gunmen stepped forward. After slapping his pistol in its holster, he balled up his fist and sent it crashing down into Jeremiah's jaw. The force of the blow rocked Jeremiah nearly out of his chair and when he glared up at the man who'd hit him, he found the gunman standing over him with his fist cocked and ready to deliver the next strike.

Brody took in the sight with mild amusement. When he saw that Jeremiah was struggling to control himself, Brody nodded to his hired gun and watched as the other man pounded Jeremiah's face a second time.

"That'll do, Marcus," Brody said. Leaning in closer to Jeremiah, he whispered, "I guess you forgot how much I hate to be talked to like that."

Rather than say what was on his mind, Jeremiah took in a haggard breath and spat a wad of blood onto the floor. His jaw was sending jolts of pain through his skull and all the way down the back of his spine every time he so much as thought about moving it. It wasn't broken, however. He'd been in enough fistfights to know that much.

Marcus stepped away from the table and rubbed his bloodied fist. He wasn't the biggest of Brody's men by far, but he was the most anxious to get a piece of the prisoner before anyone beat him to it. Moving back, he almost seemed disappointed that he hadn't taken better advantage of his opportunity.

Jeremiah choked back the blood that ran down into his throat. It tasted hot and bitter, but not nearly as much so as this whole damn situation tasted to him the more he thought about it. After all these years of working to build a better life for himself and his wife, he thought he'd come so far from the man that he'd been.

Especially when his children came into the world, Jeremiah knew that he was even less of the man that he'd left behind in the dusty past. For so long after he'd gotten married, he'd refused to plant any roots or even get too attached to whatever town he'd called home. Even when Jenny had become pregnant with Kyle, Jeremiah hadn't been ready to accept the fact that he could truly enjoy his new life.

But all that changed when he'd first seen his boy's newborn face. That was the day he not only savored the changes within himself that had been made, but truly embraced them. He saw the old Jeremiah Garver as a dead man. Therefore, the new one had to have a chance to grow into his life.

That had been nearly fourteen years ago, but it seemed like the first day of his life. Jeremiah had allowed himself to not only forge ahead as the newly created husband and father, but he'd actually done things that his old self would have never thought possible, even laughed at if he could have gotten a glimpse into this future.

He'd built a house and started herding animals. He'd gone to town to buy his food, passing the saloons along the way without even feeling the temptations of old that would have pulled him in quicker than a lasso around his body. And he'd let his gun become dusty in its holster. The only time he ever drew anymore was to put down a sick animal or kill the occasional snake.

It felt good to be the new man. Already, Jeremiah knew he was going to miss that person.

TEN

"It's a nice place you've got here," Brody said, as though he knew exactly what was going through Jeremiah's brain. "Secluded, quiet, easy to defend. I'll bet you've got enough supplies to put us all up for a few weeks."

Jeremiah felt a laugh come up from his throat like something he'd gagged up from a previous meal. "This is my home, Brody. Not a fort."

"Well, you know what they say about old habits. They die hard. Just like me."

"That's right," Jeremiah said. "I heard you met your maker up in Missouri."

"Nearly did. Plenty of nasty business up in them parts." Brody had taken to pacing in front of the widows as he talked. His movements were restless and shifty, just as Jeremiah remembered. "As much as I like it, I didn't come here to admire your house."

"Finally," Jeremiah sighed. "You come to the point."

"I sure do. You ever do much traveling anymore? I mean, besides headin' into town for grain and supplies?" That last sentence came out of Brody's mouth dripping with sarcasm and tainted with a backwater accent that made his men laugh amongst themselves.

Jeremiah caught the humor at his expense, but ignored it. "Not much. Not anymore."

"There's a town in Kentucky by the name of Haddle-ville. Ever hear of it?"

Closing his eyes, Jeremiah nodded slowly. He clenched his teeth together, which brought another significant jolt of pain from his jaw.

"I'm not surprised," Brody continued. "Especially since the bank there takes in the payrolls of every mining and railroad operation in that part of the state along with nearly every state that shares a border with it."

"That place is a robber's pipe dream," Jeremiah said. "Even in our best days the gang couldn't hit a place like that. It's too big and every guard there knows damn well that every outlaw in the country who's ever thought about hitting a bank knows what goes on in there. Besides, that money you're talking about isn't all there at once. And when it is there, it's out again in a matter of days."

Brody nodded respectfully and smiled without a trace of smugness in his features. Instead, he looked at Jeremiah as though he was looking at a friend he'd thought to be long dead. There was genuine admiration in his voice when he said, "You know an awful lot about that place for a simple family man, Jeremiah."

Letting out a slow breath, Jeremiah lowered his head and pinched his eyes shut. At that moment, he didn't know what made him hate Brody more: what he'd done to his home and children or the fact that he still knew him so well. "I'm a changed man," he said through the pain the wracked his jaw as well as his soul.

"Sure, Jeremiah. But you were too good at your job to let everything you were fall away. Those old habits of yours haven't died at all, have they?" He paused for a second to stand in front of Jeremiah and look him squarely in the eye. "You don't have to answer me. I can see I'm right just by lookin' at you.

"Be honest," Brody said while kneeling down to Jeremiah's eye level. "You've never been able to shake the feeling of riding with me and the gang. Why the hell would you want to? How could you replace the feelin' of storming into a bank with guns blazing and taking whatever the hell you want while everyone else just stands by and watches with those stupid expressions on their faces?

"Once a man feels that enough, it either kills him or soaks into his blood. For a while, I thought it might have killed you. But once I got wind that you were well and good, living here with some woman and a bunch of kids, I knew I had to come and get you so's I could save you from all those second thoughts you've been having about leaving the way you did."

Jeremiah's eyes turned into steely, burning orbs. "There ain't one doubt in my head that I did the right thing."

Reaching out with one extended finger, Brody swiped the cut in the corner of Jeremiah's mouth. "You ain't dead, so riding with me and my bunch didn't kill ya. That means you've got the fast life in your blood. I always knew you had it in there." He nodded slowly while rubbing his fingers together, squeezing the crimson fluid between them until it ran down to his knuckle. "I can feel it."

Staring into Brody's eyes, Jeremiah forgot about all the other gunmen standing inside his home and patrolling his property. He even managed to push back the fears he had concerning his children, if only for the immediate time being. When he opened his mouth, he didn't feel any of the pain from his wounded jaw. After all, the man that he used to be would never let something so insignificant keep him from doing anything. "Just because I know about Haddleville doesn't mean I want to ride in there and crack that bank open. Doing that's a death sentence. You know that just as well as I do."

"Not for you," Brody replied. "You're already dead."

He lifted his bloody fingers to his nose and took a quick sniff. When he did, his brow wrinkled as though he'd caught a whiff of something foul. "You're rotting from the inside out . . . just like all them other folks who stand by and work their lives away trying to scrape together enough money to feed them and theirs. They just sit in their holes and wait for someone to throw the dirt in while men like us go out and pull the life out of the world to make it our own."

"Why are you still preaching to me, Brody? You've got my kids and I said I'd do what you want. What more do you expect from me?"

Jeremiah half expected Brody to throw himself into another fit of rage. In fact, he could already see the frustration building up inside him until it made the corners of his eyes twitch with the strain of holding it all back. But rather than make any more threats or draw any more blood, the gang leader stared at him for another few seconds and then backed up a step.

"All I wanted was to know that the Jeremiah Garver I knew and respected was still alive," Brody said while wiping his fingers on Jeremiah's shirt. "And you just gave that to me."

ELEVEN

Standing with his back pushed tightly against the wall of the house, Clint waited for the next guard to come walking along. So far, he'd been lucky enough to drop two of the men in quick succession without making any more noise than a few steps and the dull thuds of his Colt's handle upon their knotted brows.

Clint didn't expect his luck to hold out for all four of the guards, but he was definitely more confident now that two of them had already been taken care of. The men moved in precisely timed patterns, which betrayed the fact that they were not new to their jobs. In fact, they moved a lot like trained soldiers who valued pinpoint timing and exact coordination.

Something as simple as sentry patterns told a lot about the way a gang worked. Simple bandits went for brute force and intimidation when going about their business. They relied on sheer numbers and their quick trigger fingers as their biggest assets and didn't have the patience for organized patrols, especially when guarding something like a home as remote as this one.

By simply watching the guards in action and working around their style and patterns, Clint was able to get a handle on them as he worked at taking out their outer perimeter. But all the while, he knew in the back of his mind that he could easily have missed another group of men who'd been watching him just as closely as he'd been watching the rest.

It was a very intricate game, but one with high stakes. That's the way it always went whenever men chose to play by the rules of the gun instead of the rules that applied to everyone else.

Clint thought about all of this as he listened to the next set of approaching footsteps. Just like before, he kept his breaths slow and controlled. His muscles waited without so much as a waver until the exact moment he lunged from where he'd been hiding to strike at the guard who turned the corner.

This time, there was no surprised look on the other man's face. The guard didn't pull back or fumble with his gun like the first two. Instead, he seemed to be prepared for Clint's attack, even if he didn't know exactly where or when it would come.

Swinging with the Colt in his fist, Clint saw that his target was going to duck before the handle of the pistol could make contact with his skull. In response, Clint tried to pull his swing downward, but was still unable to deliver any kind of strike before he pounded against the corner of the house.

Although the sound wasn't anything more than a dull, solid thump, it sounded louder than a gunshot in Clint's ears and he fully expected it to bring down all of the gang on top of him at any second. Until that time, however, he committed himself to bringing down this one man who was already twisting his body to get himself facing Clint.

The guard carried a rifle in his hands and because he was so close to his target, his first impulse was to bury the rifle's stock into Clint's gut with every bit of strength in his arms. Clenching his teeth together in a vicious snarl, he pivoted his upper body while delivering a sharp jab using both elbows.

Fighting to stay one step ahead of his opponent, Clint knew it was too late to avoid the incoming blow so he tensed his stomach muscles and prepared to absorb it. The stock pounded him squarely in the midsection, its upper point gouging painfully into his solar plexus. That drove a sharp spike of pain through his insides along with a good portion of the air from his lungs.

Clint still didn't have a good handle on what was going on at this house, so he was hesitant to kill any of these men. That, however, didn't mean that he was going to let himself get dropped by them. Keeping his right hand wrapped tightly around the Colt, he grabbed the guard's rifle with his left and tried to pull it from the other man's grasp.

Unwilling to be disarmed so easily, the guard tightened his grip and turned his rifle in a quick semicircle, knowing that Clint would be forced to either let go or have his wrist broken in the process. Either of those would have been just fine with him.

Clint raised his left arm a little higher until the rifle was just below his neck level. Wincing in an exaggerated show of pain, he made sure the guard thought he was hurting just enough to feed the man a sense of false security. Without overdoing it too much, Clint waited until the guard pulled back on his rifle before making his next move.

Using the momentum the guard was creating by pulling back to reclaim his rifle, Clint suddenly pushed his arm forward to drive the rifle up and out without the slightest bit of resistance from its owner. The side of the rifle smacked solidly into the guard's chin with a jarring crack. This time, the guard looked plenty surprised as his own strength was used against him to drive his own weapon into his face.

Clint made sure to hold onto the rifle as the guard flew backward and dropped to the ground in an unconscious heap. His mind was already racing with several dozen possibilities that could result from the messy and noisy way he was forced to deal with this guard. Rather than wait to see which of those possibilities would pan out, Clint holstered his Colt and rushed around the house, checking the rifle's breech as he went.

He verified that there was indeed a round in the chamber just as he came face-to-face with the fourth man who'd been walking around the outside of the house. Bringing the rifle up to his shoulder, Clint stepped forward until the weapon's barrel was touching the fourth guard on the forehead directly between his eyes.

"Tell them everything's all right," Clint whispered.

The guard looked confused for a second, his hand already tugging a pistol halfway from a holster around his waist.

Just then, the sound of the front door opening caught their attention and a rough voice shouted, "What the hell was that noise?"

Clint gave the guard a deadly stare and pushed the rifle a little harder against his skull.

"It's all right, Marcus," the guard forced himself to say. "Ford tripped, that's all."

For a second, Clint thought the bluff wasn't going to fly. Then, with a muffled grunt and a heavy slam, the door was closed and the footsteps went back inside the house. Clint didn't take the time to celebrate his luck. Instead, he snapped the rifle stock around in a quick twist of his arms to smack against the guard's temple and was gone by the time the man's back hit the dirt.

TWELVE

The sound hadn't been much. Just a thump against the side of the house. For someone used to living without any neighbors, it wasn't even anything that would have normally caused any alarm. But for someone not used to hearing an occasional animal skitter across the roof or scratching at the floorboards, it was definitely something to draw attention.

Especially when that noise came at a moment such as this one. Brody had heard the noise in the middle of his conversation with Jeremiah and his head snapped around toward that direction as though the thump had been something hitting him on the side of his own head. Even Jeremiah was distracted by it since his senses and suspicions had reverted back to those of a man who was on the lookout for anything out of the ordinary.

Brody didn't have to say anything to dispatch one of his men to check the noise. One of them automatically went to the front door and stuck his head out to investigate.

"Well?" Brody asked once Marcus walked back next to the dining table.

In response, Marcus shrugged his narrow shoulders and

46

shook his head. "He said it wasn't anything to trouble with." And that seemed to be good enough for him.

Brody's eyes narrowed and he seemed to mull that over. Instinctively, he looked toward Jeremiah as though he was wondering if that man might have had something to do with the random knock they'd all heard a minute or so ago. "Get back out there and check it yourself," he commanded.

Marcus paused for a second, which was more than enough to draw a fierce look from his boss.

"I said go check it yourself," Brody repeated. "Or is it just me who don't see the others walking outside anymore?"

Now Marcus glanced toward the windows. First, his eyes went to the one closest to him and then to the next. When he didn't see any shapes passing by either of them, he nodded and stepped out the front door, motioning for one of the other men to come along with him.

A few of the other gunmen were also peering through the windows and straining their necks to get a better look at what was going on outside.

The tension inside the house went up several degrees in the next few seconds as the gunmen whispered amongst themselves the more they looked out through their windows. Each one of them seemed anxious to get outside and looked to Brody, waiting for the order to do just that. But rather than indulge them right away, the leader of the gang seemed content to keep them all where they were . . . at least for the time being.

Just then, all of Brody's attention was focused back on the man sitting in front of him with blood trickling down from a cracked lip and dripping off his chin.

"You're getting fidgety in your old age," Jeremiah said.

Brody nodded subtly. "We'll see about that. But I can't be too careful, even if I know for a fact you ain't got anyone out there to help you."

.

Jeremiah allowed himself a slightly painful grin. "What makes you so sure about that?"

"It's not your style. You never were too quick to put your life in anyone else's hands, so you'd be even more likely to keep to yourself since you've been trying to run and hide for a living." Brody paused for a second to let the faint sound of Marcus's footsteps drift in as they made their way quickly around the house. "I think we both know what that sound was. And I think we both know what drew those guards away from their posts. Or should I say . . . *who* drew them away."

Jeremiah struggled to staunch the flow of nightmares that suddenly came to mind. He knew that Brody was talking about his children. After all, those guards outside were keeping their eyes open for the kids. Jeremiah had heard Brody's orders to them himself and knew that their first piece of business was to get their hands on the escaped children as the main bargaining chips. More than that, he knew better than anybody that Brody was right about there being no one else around to help him. Even before he'd shaken off his former life, Jeremiah had been reluctant to share his company with gunmen and bad types.

In an attempt to distract himself from the utter help-lessness he was feeling, Jeremiah asked, "So how do you propose we get ourselves in the Haddleville bank? Anyone who cares to look into it knows that the safe can only be seen by someone who's worked there for at least five years." He laughed nervously. "Hell, some say there ain't even a safe at all. There could be a hole dug in the ground for all we know. Nobody except the bank's higher-ups have even seen it to be sure."

"Oh, there's a safe all right," Brody said. "You think I would go to all this trouble to find you if I didn't know that much for certain?"

For a moment, Jeremiah's attention truly was distracted

from his fears. "Really? How do you know that? I've never heard anyone who could be trusted say they ever saw anything but the front of the tellers' windows in that bank."

Brody nodded as a knowing smile crossed his face. It was the same smile a fisherman got when he knew he'd hooked his dinner for the evening. "I know because I've got someone on the inside. They're my eyes and ears in Haddleville and they told me enough for me to walk through every square foot of that bank blindfolded."

"And that won't help you all that much if you can't get what you came for once you got there."

Brody made the shape of a gun with his thumb and forefinger, pointed it at Jeremiah and dropped the pretend hammer. "Exactly. And that's right where you come in, old friend. I didn't have the men or the spies I needed to pull this job when we worked together. But now, I've got both and all I'm missing is the one man in my gang I've never been able to replace."

Jeremiah knew that all of this talk wasn't going to do him a bit of good. He'd ridden with Brody long enough to be certain that he wouldn't make a move like this unless he was sure to have all his affairs in order. The only thing that kept Jeremiah talking was the hope that he was buying enough time for his children to get themselves a prime hiding spot and dig in so that Brody's men had no prayer of finding them. Jeremiah himself had had more than enough experience with the kids to know that they were more than capable of doing that very thing.

THIRTEEN

The room was a long way from Stony Trail, Arkansas. Situated in a large hotel in the middle of Haddleville, Kentucky, the place was lavishly furnished and stocked with enough food and drink to last the couple inside it for the better part of a week without even having to come up for air. There was even a tub near the window that could be filled with hot water in less than an hour by calling down for one of the hotel's runners.

Everything in the room was built for comfort, from the padded chairs to the quilted four-poster bed, all the way down to the voluptuous redhead lying on top of the covers. And more than that, everything in that room was paid for by Brody Saunders.

The redhead's name was Nicole Walsh, but everyone in town knew her as Nicki. She could always be found in or around one of the town's many saloons and was easily spotted by her thick mane of long, fiery hair, which made her stand out in any crowd as though a lamp was shining directly upon her. She carried herself like any woman who knew exactly how much every man in the room wanted her. Nicki had mastered the art of seduction the way some might have mastered an instrument, except her instrument was her own body and she played it like a fiddle, always assuming that she had an audience whenever she was in the public eye.

But she hadn't been seen for some time. Not since she'd run across the room's other occupant, who was a man by the name of Sherman Pierce. A man of just over thirty-five years, Pierce had the ruggedly handsome good looks that made him a natural target for Nicki's attentions. He'd had his eye on her ever since he'd come into town a week and a half ago and as soon as he'd gotten her to saunter in his direction, they'd been off to find the best room they could. And once they did, they'd hardly had a reason to poke their heads out ever since.

The only thing Nicki wore was one of Pierce's button-down shirts. Reclining on the bed, she slid one of her feet up over the quilt until her knee was bent almost completely, causing the shirt to bunch up near her waist in just such a way that revealed the soft thatch of curly red hair between her legs. Only one of the buttons was fastened, which left all but the tips of her full breasts exposed in what little sunlight could make it through the room's drawn curtains.

"What day is it?" Nicki asked absently while running the tip of her finger around the edge of a wine glass she held.

Pierce only had to think for a split second before he replied, "It's Wednesday."

"I can't believe how long we've been cooped up in here. It feels like I haven't seen the outside for a year."

Pierce's face darkened somewhat, as if hearing that made him think of something less appealing than what brought the dirty smirk to Nicki's face. "I know," he said. "I should probably run some errands today. I've put everything off for long enough."

Nicki turned the corners of her mouth down in a pout while lowering her chin just a little bit. Pulling up her other knee close to her chest, she said, "Oh, don't leave me. I though we were having so much fun together."

Pierce had been standing by the window, using one finger to pull aside the curtain, which allowed him to glimpse outside the world that moved right along, going about its regular affairs. Even the reflection of Nicki in the glass was enough to make him regret even thinking about leaving, but there was something else on his mind that caused him to force his mind back on track.

"We have been having fun," he said while turning around to look at her in the flesh. "More fun than I've had in a long time, but that doesn't mean I can ignore my business here. I've got matters to attend to. Important ones."

"You talk a lot about your business and all these important things you have to do in town," Nicki said, maintaining the undeniably sexy pout in her voice. "But you never tell me what you do." Her eyes drifted down his body, taking in the sight of him while shifting her weight upon the bed. "I mean . . . I hardly know who you are."

"We have great times together," Pierce said. He walked over to the foot of the bed, reached to a small table where the bottle of wine and another glass waited for him, and helped himself to some of the expensive vintage. "What more do you need to know?"

"How long will you be in town?"

"At least another few days."

"And how much business do you have to do today? I had plans for us."

Taking a sip of the red wine, Pierce soaked in the vision of her full, sloping curves and soft, warm flesh filling the shirt he'd been wearing on the day he'd arrived in Haddleville. "Really? And do you think those plans could wait for an hour or two while I hurry up and do what I need to do?"

"I don't know," she said softly, her knees parting

slowly to give him a generous view of her moist pussy. "You tell me if you can wait."

Pierce knew the answer to that the moment he got a look at the smooth skin of her inner thighs and the soft mound between them. "It waited this long," he said. "What's a little longer?"

FOURTEEN

Pierce moved in closer to the bed, taking a sip of the wine as he did. The warm red liquid trickled down his throat, sending an expectant chill through him along the way. Although the wine wasn't the best he could have gotten, it was the same kind they'd been drinking throughout the entire length of their stay inside the hotel room and even the smell of it was enough to remind him of all the passionate times he and Nicki had spent together.

When he dropped the glass and crawled onto the foot of the bed, the smell of the wine was quickly forgotten. As he moved forward on hands and knees, Pierce could first smell the subtle hint of Nicki's perfume and then the more intoxicating musk of her own body, which caused his penis to grow rigid the instant he caught the first hint of her scent.

Smiling widely, Nicky spread her legs for him and rested her heels on Pierce's shoulders. As he moved in closer, she slid her legs along his neck and stretched them down his back, pulling him in until she felt the brush of his lips against her flesh. Nicki still held on to her wine glass with one hand while slipping the fingers of her other hand through Pierce's thick tangle of black hair.

Pierce lowered himself down onto the bed and lay on his side while kissing the inside of her thighs. Working his mouth along her smooth, fragrant skin, he flicked his tongue out occasionally to get a better taste of her. She was sweet and had the subtle taste of roses after having spent a good part of the afternoon in a bathtub mixed with rosewater. When he moved his head between her legs, Pierce let his lips graze delicately over her pubic hair, lingering there until Nicki began to squirm impatiently beneath him.

"Don't tease me," she whispered, while pulling open her shirt. "You know how much I hate when you tease."

But she wasn't fooling him. After spending so much time together that they'd both almost lost track of it completely, Pierce knew her body almost as well as his own. He'd licked every last inch of her and ran his fingers over every bit of her flesh that he could possibly reach. He knew how much she loved to be teased and so he smirked to himself while continuing to tickle her with the fleeting touch of his mouth upon her body.

He moved along the lips of her vagina and allowed himself the luxury of sliding his tongue along the tender flesh there, lapping up just the smallest bit of her juices. When he got a little higher, he pressed his lips together and wrapped them around her clitoris, which protruded slightly from the dark red thatch of hair. As soon as he made contact with the nub of pink skin, he felt her legs tighten around his head and her fingers tighten within the hair she'd suddenly grabbed.

"Oh god, yes," she moaned. "You know just how I like it. Lick me there."

As much as he wanted to taste her some more, Pierce knew from experience just how richly he could be rewarded by torturing Nicki just a little more before giving in to her demands. Sliding his hands up over her hips,

Pierce moved his mouth away from her clit and began kissing a trail up along her stomach.

Despite the groans of protest she let out, Nicki was also moaning with pleasure enough to let him know that she was enjoying every one of those kisses just as much as Pierce was in giving them. In fact, the moment he moved within reach, Nicki slipped her hand between his legs and began stroking his cock until it was thick and rigid in her grasp.

Pierce was looking down at her breasts by now and he paused for a second to truly admire their beauty. Nicki's body was impressive enough when it was wrapped in the fine clothing she was known to wear, but when it was bare and laid out below him, Pierce had to consider it legendary.

The mounds of her breasts were full and womanly, topped with large pink nipples that were currently hard nubs that tasted sweet and clean in his mouth. Nicki narrowed her eyes and took in a deep, hissing breath when she felt him suck on and, every once in a while, lightly bite her nipples. Her feet ran along Pierce's sides, eventually pressing down against the bed so she could lift her hips up and rub her pussy against his hard column of flesh.

Now it was Pierce's turn to groan in pleasure. He pushed his hips toward her as well, testing his own limits to see if he could resist driving his cock inside her soft, moist vagina. It took everything he had, but he somehow kept himself from giving in to nearly every instinct that cried out for gratification.

This was a little game they'd been playing with each other ever since they'd had sex the first time. Once they'd had each other initially, the remaining sessions had gotten progressively longer until eventually the days started melding into one continuous night of passion.

Pierce looked down at the perfect contours of her body

and buried his face between her breasts. Running his tongue in her cleavage, he made his way up quickly to her lips and began licking her cherry-red mouth. Nicki kissed him gently at first, but soon they were probing hungrily and allowing their hands to wander freely over the other's body.

Without consciously trying to do so, Pierce settled between her legs and slipped inside of her. Nicki let out a satisfied moan as she took him in, moving her hands down to cup his buttocks and pull him inside even further.

Burying himself inside her hot wetness, Pierce drove in as far as he could go, savoring the feel of his cock being completely enveloped by her. One of Nicki's legs snaked up to hook around the back of his waist as she leaned back and pressed her hands against his chest.

Pierce drove all the way inside of her and stayed there for a moment as he straightened his back and looked down upon the gorgeous sight beneath him. Reaching down, he rubbed her breasts and slid the palms of his hands over the front of her body until he could take hold of her hips. He then used one of his thumbs to make slow, easy circles upon her clit until Nicki's breaths started coming in quick, gasping bursts.

She clenched her eyes shut and reached up to thread her fingers through her own hair, arching her back as wave after wave of pleasure coursed throughout her body. Suddenly, she felt as though she were spinning through space as she climaxed amid a flurry of loud moans that echoed inside the suite.

Pierce was almost at the breaking point himself. Every pulse of Nicki's orgasm tightened her pussy around his shaft, massaging him in the most intimate of ways. He relished that sensation for as long as he could bear it before cupping her plump backside in both hands and lifting her hips off the bed, which allowed him to pound into her in deep, hard strokes.

The sound of their flesh coming together could barely be heard over their combined voices. Every time Pierce slammed into her, Nicki grunted loudly. She turned her face into the pillow and let out a grating scream as a second orgasm started her muscles twitching and jumping beneath her skin.

Finally, Pierce lifted her hips just a little bit more while massaging her backside with both hands. When he climaxed, he felt as though his entire body was about to explode and cool shivers drifted over his skin. He stayed inside of her even after the feeling passed, setting her down and then settling on top of her.

Nicki rubbed the toes of one foot idly along his leg, her other leg loosely entwined with Pierce's. "That was wonderful," she sighed. "Almost better than when we made love on the balcony beneath the stars."

Pierce traced a line along the side of her face, looking deep into her eyes as he said, "That'll be a tough one to beat. But that doesn't mean I'm not looking forward to trying. Unfortunately, we'll have to try again some other time." With that, he got up, moved off the bed, and started collecting his clothes.

"But I don't want you to leave," she whined.

"And I'd love to stay," Pierce said after kissing her on the forehead. "But I've got business to do and it's—"

"I know. It's very important."

FIFTEEN

Pierce took one more look at Nicki lying there on the bed and felt the same conflicting emotions he had every other time he'd tried to leave the room. As much as he wanted to shuck everything and stay put for another day, another week, maybe even another month or two, he knew that he was in Haddleville for a reason. And that reason was more important than any woman . . . no matter how beautiful she might be.

Putting the finishing touches on his shirt buttons and pulling on a finely tailored gray coat, he waved to Nicki, opened the door, and actually managed to step outside. After only seeing the outside world through his window and the occasional peek through the door to let in a maid or room service, Pierce had all but forgotten what it was like to walk all the way down the hall and climb down the stairs that led to a small bar and lobby.

The hotel was bustling with activity and fairly crawling with people. In fact, being just over two hours after suppertime, the crowds in such places were at their peak and no small amount of them were filing in and out of this hotel. Although the bar was about half the size of one found in a typical saloon, it was stocked with the finest labels and a few downright rare vintages of wine. There was a dining room in the opposite part of the building tended by one of Haddleville's best cooks, but what brought in most of the regular business were the rows of card tables taking up a large room just off the lobby.

The Mason Dixon Hotel was known throughout much of the South as one of the best gambling spots in its part of the country. Plenty of well-known cardsharps stopped through Haddleville on a regular basis thanks to the Mason Dixon. And when the money was flowing exceptionally well, the town was filled to brimming with gamblers of all calibers ranging from the locals testing their lucks to the professionals out to fleece them.

It was a rare occasion when the Mason Dixon Hotel wasn't booked to capacity and teeming with players. At the tables, you could find anything from poker to blackjack and spades to faro. But, much like any other gambling hall, the game of choice was poker.

Pierce walked through the lobby and stepped up to the end of the bar. "Water, please," he said to the bartender and waited for the tall, clean glass to be set down in front of him.

After taking a sip of the cool liquid, Pierce turned around to face the rest of the room, sorting through the multitude of faces he didn't know in an attempt to single out the few he did. The glass in his hand was almost empty when he found who he was looking for: a pair of men sitting at a card table in the middle of the room. Pierce maneuvered through the crowd, dodging every so often when a chair was pushed out into his path or someone stumbled directly in front of him while going from one game to another.

Finally, he found himself next to the men he'd spotted and announced himself by setting his drink onto the table and pulling out an empty chair. He could tell that the others at the table were concentrating on the cards in their hands and knew better than to interrupt them before the hand had been played.

Once the man to Pierce's right had managed to win the small stack of chips in the middle of the table, he raked in his money and turned to look at the newest arrival. "Well, well," he said with a thick New England accent. "Look who's finally decided to show himself. I trust you've had enough time to sample the local cuisine."

By the looks on both the men's faces, Pierce knew that neither of them were referring to anything prepared by the Mason Dixon's cook. He raised his hands and plastered on a disarmingly sheepish grin. "My apologies for keeping you waiting, gentlemen, but—"

"We haven't seen hide nor hair of you for days," the man to Pierce's left interrupted. "You're cutting it awful close, don't you think? The others will be here before you know it."

Pierce nodded respectfully and kept his hands in the air. "I'm aware of that and I assure you I'll be ready when they arrive."

"You'd better be," the first man said, his tone suddenly becoming very grave. "Because they don't have half as much patience as we do. When they pull into town, you're as good as dead if you're still up in your room fucking that whore you purchased with our money."

Pierce didn't even flinch at the profanity. Instead, he lowered his hands and put on an equally severe expression. "I told you I'd do what I came to do. And though I have been . . . indisposed for quite a bit of my time, that's only because things have been going even more smoothly than I'd anticipated."

That seemed to please both men and they showed this by relaxing somewhat and bobbing their heads in approval.

"Do you know when our . . . partners will arrive?" Pierce asked.

The man to his right glanced around the room as though checking for any unwanted listeners. All he found, however, was a bunch of strangers too absorbed in their cards to give a damn as to what happened in the rest of the world around them. Of course, that was exactly why they'd chosen this spot for their meeting. "Shouldn't be too much longer. How much is left to do on your end?"

Pierce shrugged off the inquiry with casual indifference. "Hardly anything at all."

"And you haven't told anyone about our schedule, have you?"

Ever since he'd been commissioned for this job, Pierce had known that discretion was a major part of it. He wasn't to speak about any of his comings or goings to anyone except those who were paying for his services. He'd been reminded about that fact more times than he cared to remember and he'd thought about it even when he and Nicki were together in the suite they'd shared.

Although he'd done his best to uphold his part of the bargain, he was only human after all and was prone to talking to whoever lay next to him in the dark. Pierce hadn't told her much . . . hardly anything at all, really, but still knew better than to admit to even the slightest slip of the tongue.

"Of course I haven't said anything about the schedule," Pierce said while all of these thoughts went through his mind. "I know better than that."

"As well you should," the man to his left grumbled. "Now, let's get out of here so you can take me on a tour of this bank I've been hearing so much about. I trust you've scouted it out and are ready to give a report."

"Sure thing, gentlemen," Pierce said while pushing away from the table. "If you'll just follow me."

SIXTEEN

"I'm scared, Kyle." Sadie's words drifted through the air like a fragile piece of ice that was half a second away from breaking upon the surface of a thawing stream. Her voice wavered slightly and could barely be heard over the slowly rustling wind.

Kyle lay on his stomach on the top of the ridge, his eyes barely visible between the crisscrossing branches of the bushes they used for cover. "I know," he said to his sister without looking back at her. "I am too."

After a few more seconds went by, Sadie crawled between the branches without making the slightest sound. Even being as scared as she was didn't take away from her natural skill at the deadly game she and her brother were playing. "Can you see anything?"

Squinting through the branches, Kyle wrinkled his brow in concentration and nodded slowly. "I saw that man go down there and almost get caught."

"Clint."

"What?"

"His name was Clint," Sadie said in the condescending voice that never failed to get on her brother's nerves. "That's what he told us."

"Whatever. He got down there and beat those men quicker than you could blink. I saw it."

Sadie let out a disappointed whine. "I wish I had." Moving up a little closer to Kyle's side, she asked, "Where is he now?"

"He went around the house and then came back again. I think he got them other men, but I couldn't see so well from all the way up here. After that, he took off toward the shed."

Looking down on the house, Sadie was just in time to see more of Brody's men come pouring out from the front door and bark gruff orders to each other. "Oooo, he's in trouble!"

Kyle twisted around to glare at the little girl. Clamping one hand over her mouth, he used his other to swat her lightly on the top of her head. "I told you before to be quiet," he whispered. "Pa said to stay hid and not let anyone find us."

Sadie rubbed at the spot where her brother had smacked her, but didn't make another sound. By the look on her face, one might have thought she'd been knocked senseless, but she quickly recovered and seemed to forget the blow in the space of a few seconds.

"You see that?" Kyle said while pointing toward a group of figures moving together away from the house. "Them are the men that was chasing Clint."

At first, there were only three of them moving toward the small shed built on the edge of the Garvers' property. But as both children watched, they spotted two more join the group and move in toward the shed. Before they got too close, the gunmen fanned out and started to surround the small building with guns drawn.

Glancing nervously over her shoulder, Sadie pushed in closer to Kyle's side. "What about that man back there by them horses?"

"Clint said not to worry about him . . . but I want to check it out for myself."

"No," Sadie whined, her little hand wrapping tightly around Kyle's forearm. "We have to stay here. They'll find us!"

Kyle jerked his arm free in one quick motion. "Hush up and stay put. They won't see anything so long as you keep quiet. I'll be right back."

And before Sadie could say another word in protest, her brother was already gone. Since she knew what to look for, she could just make out the shape of Kyle's body wriggling through the brush. He moved like a snake, which was the exact same way he moved whenever he crept up and scared her all those countless times since she could remember.

Sadie had always hated him for all the tricks he pulled on her and all the ways he scared the wits out of her any chance he got. But watching him now, she could only be scared for him. Silently, she said a prayer for her brother, hoping that he would come back and tell her where to go and what to do. She also said one for her father and by the time she was finished, Kyle was creeping back to her side.

"That was no lie," the young boy said while catching his breath. "That man we saw back there is tied up like a pig."

Both children covered their mouths to keep from making too much noise as they laughed at that image. Also, the relief they felt at not having to worry about the closest stranger helped lighten their mood somewhat.

"So we can wait here for Poppa just like we were supposed to?" Sadie asked hopefully.

Staring down at the men who'd now completely surrounded the shed, Kyle took in a deep breath and shook his head. "Nope. I'm gonna help Clint."

"How!?"

"I don't know," he said while crawling forward toward the edge of the ridge. "But I gotta try."

Kyle slithered on his belly along a track in the dirt that only he and his sister knew was there. Looking back over his shoulder just before coming out of the bushes, he saw that Sadie was pressed with her nose almost to the ground, getting ready to follow. He started to wave her back, but then remembered the times when he and his sister had gotten lost and Pa had praised him for being smart enough to stay close to his sister so they could both be found together.

Rather than take the time to scold her yet again, Kyle waved for her to join him and they both worked their way along the edge of the ridge, keeping their small bodies as close as possible to the bushes. They'd played this game hundreds of times, only the bandits they'd been trying to hide from back then had been imaginary while these were all too real.

They crept through the brush and were quickly over the spot that looked down on their father's shed. Kyle could see that every one of the men standing outside the shed were carrying guns and by the sound of their voices, they were awfully mad about something.

"What do we do now?" Sadie's voice was just loud enough for Kyle to hear. Her movements were so light that he'd almost forgotten about her completely.

"You watch for Pa. I'll . . . I'll think of something."

SEVENTEEN

Jeremiah could tell by the frustration building in Brody's voice that his tolerance with this conversation was growing short. More than likely, he knew exactly what Jeremiah was trying to do, but if his men were unable to find the kids, there wasn't a damn bit of good that knowledge would do.

"What about the law?" Jeremiah asked. "They're ready to swarm down on that bank at a moment's notice. What do you propose to do about them?"

Shrugging, Brody replied, "Won't have to do anything about them so long as we're quick about it. The law's bought and paid for. Forget about them."

"But things hardly ever go that smoothly. Even I know that much."

"These ain't even half of my gang," Brody said while idly pointing to the men around him. "There's plenty more waiting for us over the Arkansas line and they'll be more than enough to hold off an army of law dogs if the roof caves in on us. But even if it does, we'll still get out as rich men. Even your cut will be enough to set you up for life."

Jeremiah could hear a commotion outside, punctuated

by the gruff voices of several of Brody's gunmen. He tried
not to let the desperate fear in his heart show through
when he nodded and said, "Fine. I'm in. But only if you
call your men in . . . right *now*."

Brody's eyes narrowed suspiciously and he cocked his
head as a distasteful look drifted onto his face.

"You stop looking for my kids," Jeremiah continued.
"Let them go, or I'll die before I help you pull this job.
And if I know you like I think I do, you didn't come here
unless you failed after searching high and low for anyone
else as good as me. I'm no good to you dead . . . so take
it or leave it."

Jeremiah knew he was gambling with his life. And for
a brief moment, he thought he might have just pushed his
offer too far.

At that moment, the front door burst inward and one
of Brody's head guards stepped inside.

Brody glanced over his shoulder, being careful to keep
Jeremiah in the corner of his eye at all times. "What is it,
Ford?"

The guard had a sunken face with features that looked
as though they'd been drawn onto him by an inept sketch
artist. His eyes were particularly dim and his hair hung
down over his forehead in a way that made him look like
a shaggy dog. "Marcus sent me to tell you that someone
got by me and the others."

Brody's face twisted into an almost distorted mask of
sheer rage. "What the *hell* did you just say to me?"

Ford instinctively took a step back, but stopped just
short of actually leaving the house. "He didn't hurt none
of us too bad . . . and we got him cornered outside."

"Who? Who didn't hurt you?"

"Hell if I know." Suddenly, Ford's dull face lit up and
he hefted a chubby finger toward Jeremiah. "Ask him. It's
probably someone he knows that's trying to come help
him out of here."

Brody looked across the table just in time to see Jeremiah shrug convincingly. "Whoever he is, just find him and kill him. We ain't got the time to be messing with this bullshit!"

Ford nodded once and walked outside, letting the front door slam in his wake. His footsteps hurried off the porch and soon dropped onto the ground to rush off in the direction of the shed.

"Do you know anything about this?" Brody asked.

Jeremiah allowed himself a little smile. "Would you believe me one way or another however I answered that question?"

"Probably not. It don't matter one way or the other since whoever it is will be dead in the space of another minute or two." Brody watched Jeremiah's face for any kind of reaction to that statement. He saw no trace of hope upon hearing about this other man or regret at the notion that he might be dead. All of that made him think that Jeremiah might just be telling the truth after all.

"My offer still stands," Jeremiah said. "Call off the hunt for my children and I'll come along with you on this job. Harm so much as a hair on their heads and the deal's off. You can try your luck in finding someone else with my qualifications."

"There ain't nobody else," Brody admitted.

"True enough."

For a few seconds, the only sound in the house was the angry voices barking orders to each other outside. The guards' curses and commands drifted in through the windows and doors like a passing breeze, sending a chill down Jeremiah's spine.

Finally, Brody slapped the table with his open palm and let out a booming laugh. "This is why I always liked you, Garver. No matter how badly it was all stacked against you, there was always some way for you to turn everything around so that you had the upper hand. Hell, I might even cut you in on the money just for old time's sake."

"I don't give a shit about your money," Jeremiah said plainly. "What about my children?"

"If you're willing to come along with us to Haddleville, then I couldn't give a rat's ass about them kids."

"Then it's a deal?"

"Yeah," Brody said with a nod. "It's a deal."

"Then call off your men before they hurt my son or daughter." When he heard some of the guards yelling excitedly to one another, Jeremiah couldn't keep the worry from showing on his face. Once again, he was picturing all the horrific things that might be happening to Kyle or Sadie while he sat here shooting the breeze with this son of a bitch. "Call them off now!"

"Don't fret yourself," Brody said with deliberate calm. "If they'd found your kids, I would've known about it. But I'll go out and check all the same." Getting back to his feet, he moved toward the door and stopped with his hand wrapped around its handle. "But be sure about one thing, if I so much as get the idea that you're fixin' to double-cross me on this . . . I'll track them brats down if it takes me the rest of my life . . . and I'll gut them like freshly killed venison."

He was out the door in the next second, leaving Jeremiah with an even heavier weight sitting upon his shoulders.

EIGHTEEN

As Clint was running for the shed, he'd been hoping to draw off a few of the other guards that might be posted around the house. That way, he'd figured on getting a better idea on just how many more there truly were and where they'd taken up their positions.

That hastily conceived plan brought about a good news/bad news scenario. The good news was that he now had a real good idea of how many more men were ready to respond to the fallen guards. The bad news was that most of those men were coming after him with everything they had, without being too concerned about anything else but killing Clint as fast as they possibly could.

While Clint hadn't fooled himself into thinking that this would be easy, he had thought that at least some of the remaining guards would remain at their posts just in case there was anybody else coming. Apparently, they knew enough about the area and the man living in that house to know that even the law was no threat to them out here.

Clint's original plan was to make whatever men were pursuing him think that he was going to hide out in the shed, when actually he would come out through a back door he'd spotted earlier and make his way back up to the children. The guards were supposed to waste some time looking for him, which would have allowed Clint to get back to Eclipse and then approach the house from another angle entirely.

It had seemed like a good idea at the time. But now that he'd found out the hard way that the guards were a little more anxious than even he'd expected, it seemed it was time to think of a new plan. Silently cursing himself for not taking more time to think things through, Clint knew deep down inside that he didn't have the time for such luxuries. Besides, it was never too late for a little creative thinking.

The moment Clint ducked inside the shed, he noticed that there was a wooden plank set next to the door that could be fit into a pair of brackets on either side. Although the wood looked sturdy enough, the fact that it was there gave Clint a sudden burst of hope that this might not have been such a bad idea after all.

If the door was set up to be locked from the inside, that meant that there had to be another way out. Clint slapped the plank into place just as he heard the sound of footsteps coming, followed by several voices of guards issuing whispered orders to one another. He then made his way to the back door, nearly tripping over various tools and stacks of lumber scattered along the floor.

Pausing for no more than a second, Clint pressed his ear to the back door and listened to see if he could hear anything just outside. From what he could tell in that fleeting moment, the guards were being cautious as they circled the shed, preparing themselves for whatever Clint might have in store for them.

Clint was just about to make a break for it when he spotted the very thing he'd been looking for: another set of brackets on either side of the door as well as a plank similar to the one propped up at the front of the shed. His next moment was spent scanning the shed for the only thing he could think of that might also be in a shack built to be locked from the inside.

He found that thing as soon as he heard that the guards had surrounded him. And when he did, a wry grin drifted across his face.

"You boys ready?" Marcus called out to the gunmen who'd positioned themselves around the back of the shed.

He got a response in the form of a quick wave from the other side of the rickety building. Once he saw that, he cocked back the hammer of his pistol and nodded to the guard standing at his side. "Go try that door," he ordered. "The rest of you in back . . . be ready . . . now!"

With that, the men at the front and back doors smashed into them with their boots and were immediately shaken to their bones by the jarring impact when neither door gave way. That didn't hold either of them for long and when they tried again, another man helped on either side, lending their shoulders to the effort as once again, bodies smashed upon lumber.

The entire shed rocked slightly at the double barrage, shaking dust and small pebbles loose from where they'd been lodged in the shingles and rafters. This time, although the front door remained solid, the men in the back managed to break through and let out a victorious shout.

Hearing this, Marcus rushed toward the side of the shed, turning to issue more commands as he went. "Two of you stay right there and get him if he gets flushed out this way," he said. And before he could get any replies from his men, he was headed toward the shed's back door.

There were already three men crowded at the opening, holding pistols and rifles at the ready, pointing them into the musty darkness. One of them saw that Marcus had arrived and stepped back to let him through. Most of the door swung back and forth on its hinges, while the rest of it lay propped up in the frame to reveal the shattered plank that had been broken on impact. Besides the beams of light filtering in from the cracked door and the occasional flaw in the walls, there wasn't much to see besides a lot of blocky shapes.

"You sure he's in there?" one of the men asked.

Marcus looked like he'd been about to ask the same question. When he glanced around at the faces of the men gathered round, he got a few nods from some of those who'd called the others out.

One of them was one of the guards who'd been knocked on the head by the stranger and he wore a nasty red knot on his forehead to prove it. When Marcus saw that one nod as well, he stood back and lifted his pistol.

"All right, then," he said while taking aim at a shape in the dark. "Let's get what we came for."

After he fired his first shot, all the others standing next to him did the same. They blasted everything they could see inside the shed along with several things they couldn't. And they didn't stop firing until they had to stop and reload.

Nothing could survive inside that storm of lead, Marcus knew. But just to be sure . . .

"Spread out," he said to the men around him. "Give the others some space." And then, waving to the men at the front of the shed, he stood back and let them blow it apart from their end.

NINETEEN

For the next minute or two, it was impossible to see anything inside the shed besides soupy gray smoke churning around amid the shadows like a writhing demon. The light inside the small building had doubled thanks to all the new holes that had been blown through the walls, but that somehow didn't help much in the guards' attempts to find what they were looking for inside.

Every one of them had reloaded their weapons and were standing in position, waiting for the slightest hint of movement that they could still by another barrage of gunfire. For his part, Marcus felt like he wanted to tear the place apart with his bare hands. It was bad enough that one man had made fools of his men, but now that same man was holding them all off when there was real business to take care of.

"You," Marcus said, pointing to the gunman closest to the back door. "Get in there and see what you can find."

Without the slightest hesitation, that man thumbed the hammer back on his pistol and walked into the smoky shadows. The acrid mist chewed at the back of his throat and inside his nose like hundreds of tiny claws. He waved his hand in front of his face while stepping into the shed, stirring up the gun smoke with every pass of his hand.

His nerves were at the ready and the adrenaline was already pumping through his veins after hearing the massive amount of gunfire that had turned this shed into a sieve. For a moment, he swore he saw a body lying crumpled on the floor, but when he kicked it with the toe of his boot, he realized it was only an old tarp rolled into a bulky tube.

"What was that?" came a voice so suddenly that it caused every man in or near the shed to turn toward it with their guns raised.

The man who'd said it was not looking toward the shed, but was actually glaring up at the land away from all of the buildings. At first, the others simply looked at each other and shrugged to draw their own conclusions about what might have caused the outburst. But then, a different man felt something crack him on the side of his head.

Wheeling around to look, the second man almost fired before setting his eyes on a good target. "Shit! I felt something hit me!"

"You felt it too?" the first guard asked, rubbing a spot on his brow where a small trickle of blood was meandering down his face. "This bastard's playing with us."

Marcus watched all of this while shaking his head in disbelief. It didn't take long for that feeling to be replaced by frustration and then murderous anger. "Jesus Christ. Someone go and see what the hell is going on." Turning to the man who still stood inside the shed, he snarled, "Tear that place apart just to be sure. I'm checking back in with Brody and the owner of this shit hole."

Three of the guards stayed at the shed while the rest of them spread out onto the rest of the property, jumping at nearly every noise they heard or even made by the press of boots against dry twigs. Marcus stormed back to the house, his eyes constantly searching for the stranger he hated even though he'd never even seen him.

• • •

Ford Fargo was just on his way out from talking to Brody when he'd been ordered to search the rest of the property. Although he wasn't exactly sure what had been going on to spread all the men so thin, that wasn't an unfamiliar feeling for Ford, who'd gotten used to being in the dark for most of his life.

Now, he drew his gun and started walking the property, glancing around as though he knew what he was looking for. Just then, he heard the sound of something whipping through the air, coming at him from behind. When he turned, he caught a glimpse of something gray and solid right before it bounced off the center of his forehead.

Pain lanced through his head, causing Ford to reach up and press his free hand against the fresh wound. "Awww, shit," he grunted.

One of the men closest to him turned and looked. "You get hit? What the f—" was all he could get out before another object sped through the air and thumped against that guard's chest. Although it didn't hurt as much as if he'd caught the thing in the face like the other two, the impact was enough to startle the guard and spin him around like a top while he searched for the source of the shot.

While he couldn't find where the thing had come from, he did see another one as it dropped from the sky to crack him squarely on the collar bone. That time, the guard felt his share of pain. It wasn't nearly enough to put him down, but it stirred up the anger in him the way a badly placed stick might stir up a beehive.

Looking down at the ground near his feet, the guard searched for and quickly found the thing that had struck him. He bent at the knees and swiped it up in a thick paw of a hand. The stone was nothing special; just flat, gray, and small enough to disappear when the guard closed his fist around it. Even so, that rock pissed off the big man even more than if it had been a bullet.

"Son of a bitch is throwin' rocks at us," the guard hollered. Thinking back to the arc of the rock's fall, he pointed toward a clump of nearby bushes. "And it came from that way!"

That was all the rest of the guards needed to hear. They all took off toward those bushes at a dead run, even as another rock spun through the air and slapped against Ford's chin. Each of the guards running in that direction saw the rock arc through the air and turned to rush in that direction. A couple of them fired off a shot or two into the bushes before the first one reached the spot.

"He's here somewhere," Ford shouted.

The bigger guard stopped short of charging into the brush and started searching through the bare branches. "He's probably tryin' to lead us away from the shed into some kind of ambush, so keep yer eyes open and shoot at the first thing that moves."

At that moment, all of the guards stopped walking and looked carefully into the brush. Before too long, one of them snapped his fingers and pointed toward a spot near one of the farther bushes. Something was moving. In the next instant, that something had no fewer than three gun barrels pointed directly at it.

TWENTY

Clint crouched where he was hiding and strained his ears, listening to the footsteps clomping around him. The noise seemed to wrap around his entire body and shake him like an impatient father's hand. But just when he thought they were going to get closer, the steps moved back and actually started to fade away.

For a moment, he thought his ears might be playing tricks on him. But it didn't take long for him to be certain that he had, indeed, heard correctly. The men searching for him were moving away, although he could still hear voices nearby.

The moment for his escape had to be chosen perfectly since he would not be able to get another one if he botched the first. So rather than storm ahead before he was absolutely certain, Clint waited for another few seconds until his instincts told him it was time to go.

Marcus stood at the rear of the shed and pounded his fist against the wall. "What the hell is goin' on here?" he shouted. "I just got back from talking to Brody and he looked like he was about to swap spit with that farmer we tracked down to this piece of backwoods land."

79

"That's no farmer," replied another guard. "He used to work with Brody in the old days. He's the best—"

"I don't give a shit who he is. My point is that Brody still thinks everything's going just fine. He said to hold off looking for them kids and get everyone to track down this other bastard who walked through my men."

"Did you tell him we lost that one?"

Turning to glare at the guard with fire in his eyes, Marcus had to force himself not to send his fist into the guard's face. "No . . . because we didn't lose him. He's on the run somewhere in them hills throwin' rocks like some damn . . ." Just then, Marcus's eyes widened as a light seemed to go on behind his eyes. ". . . like some damn kid! Holy shit, I don't believe—"

Before he could get the rest of his sentence out, Marcus heard something coming from the shed directly behind him. It sounded like a door opening although he could see through the back door, which was already open, all the way to the front door, which wasn't even moving. Instead, the door that had opened was a square trapdoor in the floor, which more than likely led down to a storage cellar and was all but invisible in the dim, dusty light within the shed.

As soon as they saw the movement inside the shed, it was too late for them to do anything to stop Clint as he emerged from beneath the floor and charged forward like a rampaging bull. Marcus's first instinct was to jump to one side and draw his gun, but the guard next to him caught the full brunt of Clint's charge, which drove all the air from his lungs and almost knocked him clean out of his boots.

Clint let out a rumbling growl as he rushed toward both men, uncertain as to whether or not he was throwing himself into a storm of lead or even a group of men who'd been standing around waiting for him. All he knew was that his gut had told him to make his play and he wasn't about to start questioning his instincts after all these years of having them save his life time and time again.

When Clint's shoulder pounded into the first guard, he kept running a few more steps while wrapping his arms around the man's midsection just to be sure he put the guy down. Clint threw his weight into the last few steps and slammed the guard into the soil. When he saw the dazed look on that one's face, he whirled around to face the second man he'd seen.

Marcus was waiting for him, sighting down the barrel of a .44 and taking careful aim. Without saying a word, he squeezed the trigger and sent a round of hot lead screaming through the air toward Clint's chest.

But Clint had outguessed the other man at the last second and was already in the process of diving to one side when the .44 went off. The bullet flew over his head, missing him by less than an inch or so before passing into the nearby bushes.

Tucking his chin against his chest, Clint threw himself into a tight forward roll and came up on both feet. He spun around and drew the modified Colt in one fluid motion, drawing a bead on his target and then firing. The entire process took less than two seconds and he'd taken his shot before Marcus had a chance to cock back the hammer of his .44 a second time.

Clint's shot hissed through the air and dug a bloody trench through Marcus's wrist. Sheared flesh peeled back in both directions amid a spray of blood, causing Marcus to reflexively let go of his weapon just as he was about to fire. The pistol thumped to the ground near his feet and he grabbed for the fresh wound with his free hand.

Knowing that the sound of the shots would attract attention, Clint moved forward and kicked away the fallen pistol. He then turned around just as the other guard was struggling to get up. Clint's boot came around in a snapping half circle to catch that guard on the chin and send him back to the ground.

Clint was able to see the remaining guards fanned out around the property and could even hear shots coming from a different area. He hoped the children had had enough sense to keep themselves out of harm's way and ran over to the main house.

After coming all this way and going through all this trouble, he wasn't about to leave without seeing just what was going on. He covered the distance between the shed and the house in a matter of seconds. Even though some of the shots were starting to be aimed at him, he kept on running until he was able to jump onto the porch and smash through the front door.

In an instant, Clint took in the scene within the house. There were two men sitting at a table and another one guarding them from the corner of the room. The one guard looked surprised, but was still going to try and take a shot at Clint. He wouldn't be nearly fast enough to get that done; before he could get a shot off, Clint's pistol bucked in his hand and drilled a hole through the guard's shoulder. The wound wasn't fatal, but it was more than enough to put that gunman down.

"You!" Clint said, pointing to one of the men at the table. "Get up and come with me."

TWENTY-ONE

Clint didn't give the man a chance to voice any of the concern that showed in his eyes. By the looks of him, the man was just as confused as the rest, but wasn't hesitant to get to his feet as Clint came thundering by. Having spotted the back door at the other end of the room, Clint took the man by the wrist and dragged him toward the other door, kicking it open the moment his legs could reach it.

"What's going on?" the man asked breathlessly. "Who are you?"

Clint kept running until he and his temporary hostage were in the midst of a thick bunch of bushes. For the moment, the guards were spread out on the opposite end of the property and it would take them a minute or so to figure out exactly where Clint had gone.

"I'm not one of them and I'm not the law either," Clint said quickly. "But I'm guessing you're in a bit of trouble."

The man looked back at him in utter disbelief. "How do you know me?"

"I don't, but I was told there was trouble this way. When I came in to check it out, I nearly got shot up myself. And when I managed to get inside that house, you

struck me as the one man in there who was in the most
need of assistance."

A few shots were fired close by, but they were still a
little ways off. The man wasn't trying to escape, but he
still seemed shocked. "And how did you pick me out in
the second you were standing there?"

"Easy," Clint said. "You're not wearing a gun belt."

Jeremiah looked down and shook his head. "I'll be
damned. Did you see my children on the way down here?"

"Two boys?" Clint said without missing a beat. "One
blond and another with black hair?"

"No . . . a boy and a girl."

"What are their names?"

"Sadie and Kyle," the man replied without hesitation.

Nodding, Clint said, "Just a little test. They're all right.
They were hidden pretty well farther up the ridge. Now
let's get out of here and we can straighten this all out
once we're safe. There are some horses up where I
found—"

"I can't go."

"What?" Clint turned to look at the house and saw some
of the guards working their way closer to where he and
Jeremiah were hiding. "We've run out of time already.
I'm not just going to let you go back to those fellas. They
seem pretty unfriendly to me and your kids said they were
going to kill you."

Jeremiah talked quickly as he started moving back toward the house. "Look. You don't know everything going
on here. If I don't go with those men, they'll keep after
my children until they find them and they'll take out anyone who stands in their way."

"Then let me—"

"If you want to be a help, warn the bank at Haddleville,
Kentucky, about a robbery that's set to go on in the next
few days. In the meantime, get out of here and take the
children somewhere safe. Do that, and I'll see to it you

get a reward for your troubles." Before he took off, Jeremiah turned around to fix Clint with a cold, no-nonsense stare. "And if I find that you harmed those children, I'll put you through every inch of hell there is."

And with that, he was gone.

Clint watched as Jeremiah ran from the bushes in long, heavy strides, making just enough noise to be heard and plenty of noise to cover Clint's own steps as he moved off through the brush. Once he saw that Jeremiah had joined up with the gunmen and was doing his best to keep them from going any farther toward the bushes, Clint worked his way farther up until he once again started climbing the ridge.

TWENTY-TWO

"What's going on?" Brody demanded as he stormed out of the house. Apparently, he'd waited until he'd collected a few of his men to accompany him before heading after Jeremiah and Clint. "Who was that?"

Jeremiah shrugged and went back to Brody's side. "I don't know. These parts are filled with types like that who try to bust in and rob any man who's got more than two sticks to rub together."

Brody's eyes narrowed and he glanced suspiciously from Jeremiah to the surrounding brush. "He came for you and no one else. The boys say he slid through them like a greased pig."

"I'm still here, ain't I?" Jeremiah said in his defense. "If I wanted to go, I'd be gone. But you've got my word and you should know that's worth something."

"Yeah," Brody said after a few moments' consideration. "He didn't look like no law, so I guess he's not worth any more of our time. Marcus," he said, turning to the man who was rushing around the outside of the house. "Call in the others. We got what we came for."

Grudgingly, Marcus put two fingers to his lips and let

out a shrill whistle that reverberated over the property like a tortured demon. "Pack it in!" he shouted.

Brody's men started filing in from the surrounding area upon hearing the call. All but two, who were taking a little more time than the rest.

Ford Fargo and the bigger guard heard the whistle, but had almost pinpointed the source of the rocks that had been thrown at them. They could hear the rustling of the occasional branch and the shuffling of what could only be a small person or a large animal creeping through the bushes.

Both men knew it hadn't been the stranger who'd thrown the rocks, but that didn't mean they were any less intent on punishing the one who had. Ford took one more look at the ridge and swore under his breath before turning and heading for the house. His partner, however, didn't seem too eager to give up the search.

"Come on," Ford said. "You heard Marcus. The search is off."

The bigger guard bared his teeth and kept staring at the bushes. So far, they had yet to spot anyone moving through the branches, which made the noises they heard all the more infuriating. "Goddamnit!" he hollered while firing another round into the brush. With that last little bit of satisfaction, he turned on his heels and stomped back toward where Brody and the rest were gathering.

Jeremiah heard that gruff voice swearing at the top of its lungs, followed by a shot that made his shoulders jump up around his ears. Since he knew the stranger had taken off in the other direction, that meant the shot must have been fired at the other targets being hunted. Besides, he knew that frustration only too well after raising the kids on his own for most of their lives.

Wheeling around to face Marcus, Brody stepped up until he was glaring directly into the gunman's face. "I thought I told you to let those brats go!"

"You did," Marcus replied, seemingly unaffected by Brody's gruff tone. "And I told them myself. But we weren't sure it was the children who'd drawn us away from that shed. It could've been someone working with that stranger."

Brody silenced him with a quick wave of his hand while turning back to face Jeremiah. "Whatever it was they was after, they didn't get it."

Somehow, Jeremiah felt a calm feeling in the pit of his stomach. It was in that same place that had been jumping whenever he feared for his children. And it was the same place that would have been cold and empty if they'd been hurt. "Yeah," he said, strangely sure of himself. "I know."

For the next minute or two, Brody and Jeremiah watched nothing but each other. Their eyes were locked as they measured each other like a pair of wolves that were about to tear into one another. Before too long, they came to a silent agreement and they both turned to look in another direction.

Jeremiah turned to face the ridge overlooking his home. Even though he was fairly certain he wouldn't be able to spot Kyle or Sadie, he stared up at the ridge and lifted his hand in the air as though he was waving to them. The gesture wasn't much more than a flex of an arm, but it was the same motion he always used when waving to the kids whenever they were out of earshot. He could only hope they were watching for it the way he'd asked them to.

Brody stood in front of his men like a general about to address his troops. Although he saw Jeremiah's wave from the corner of his eye, he ignored it completely, thinking that he had the big advantage for the time being. "All right," he said imperiously. "I want someone to go fetch the horses and bring them down here. Once we're all saddled up, we're heading for the Kentucky state line."

"You have an extra horse for me?" Jeremiah asked.

Brody snapped his fingers, reveling in the role of commander. "Marcus, get that horse in the pen over by the house. Check the saddle for any weapons and then get it ready for our new partner here." Facing the rest of the men, Brody said, "This is Jeremiah Garver. I want everyone to treat him real nice. And if he tries to leave our company before I give the say-so . . . feel free to shoot him."

There were a few chuckles among the gunmen, but not one of them thought that Brody was kidding.

While the rest of the men went about their duties, Brody turned back to Jeremiah. "You won't regret this, old friend. In fact, when this is all over, I'll bet you'll even thank me."

"Yeah," Jeremiah said in a low voice. "We'll see about that."

TWENTY-THREE

Kyle crouched behind a particularly thick clump of bushes and sifted through the dirt to find another flat stone. After years of practice, he knew the flatter ones flew better, even though the fatter ones did more damage when they hit. Behind him, Sadie clasped both hands over her mouth to try and keep her giggling from being heard.

Despite the fact that the gunmen who'd been hit by Kyle's rocks had been getting closer and closer to finding him, the boy never seemed to be concerned. Instead, fueled by the blind courage of youth, he'd kept on the outer edge of the guards' sight so he could keep distracting them with a maddening rain of pebbles upon their heads.

"Did they catch Clint?" Sadie asked from behind her brother.

"Nope," Kyle replied. "They had him cornered in the shed, but he must've gotten out. They looked all confused, and when I started hitting them, they scattered like rabbits."

Now, both children had to struggle to keep their voices down as they relished their little victory from the safety of their hiding spot.

Suddenly, Sadie's face darkened and she cowered down

a little closer to the ground. "Did any of those men see us?"

"Hell no. They didn't even—"

"Watch your language," came a voice that nearly made both of them jump out of their skins.

Kyle turned around in a flicker of motion, cocking his fist back behind his ear, ready to hurl another rock in self-defense. Choking back a frightened squeal, Sadie dropped down and covered her head with her hands.

Before Kyle could let his rock fly, he saw the face of the man who'd just spoken. Clint was making his way toward them, crouching down low to stay out of sight. He raised his hands in surrender when he got to where the children were huddled.

"I thought I told you two to stay hidden," Clint said.

Suddenly, Kyle looked as though the only problem in his world was getting into trouble. He dropped the rock and locked his arms behind his back before saying, "I didn't mean to . . . I . . . I was only trying to help."

Clint sat down behind the children and looked over the top of the ridge from his new perch. "Don't worry. You did a fine job, but I don't want you to draw any attention right now. Understood?"

"I saw Pa," Kyle said softly. "He waved at us before those men took him away. I don't think he saw us, but he knew we'd see him."

Clint was busy watching the gunmen move around by the house in packs of two or three. He and the children were almost on the opposite side of the ridge from where he'd left them and the only way he'd been able to track them down at all was because of that one last shot taken in frustration just as the gunmen were called in by Brody.

If he didn't know exactly what to listen and look for, Clint might have passed the children by as well. But not only had he spotted them moving in the bushes, he'd heard their excited laughter, which had been like a beacon to him as he'd worked his way up the side of the incline.

"Your father's going away," Clint said. "And you can't go with him."

Kyle's response was quiet and resigned. "I know."

Clint looked down at the boy and was struck by the resolve he saw in his youthful features. "You do?"

Nodding, Kyle replied, "Yessir. Pa told me once that men might come looking for him. And if they did, I was to hide until he gave me a signal. If'n he waved at me instead, I was supposed to take Sadie and stay with our Aunt Colleen. He'll come back for us . . . after a while."

As much as he tried to hide it, Kyle was unable to keep a tear from leaking from the corner of one eye. He swiped at it with the back of his sleeve as though it stung his skin and looked down quickly to make sure Sadie hadn't spotted his indiscretion.

But the little girl was too busy staring down at the house. She took in the sight of all those men swarming around her home and muttered softly to herself.

"Tell me about your pa," Clint said to Kyle. "What did he look like?"

Although the boy seemed confused, he cocked his head and rattled off a quick description. "Tall and strong. He's got dark hair with some white by his eyes and a scar on his chin, which he told me he got from getting thrown by a horse."

Clint didn't have to hear the rest of what the boy said. The only reason he'd asked the question in the first place was to double-check that he'd spoken to the right man behind the house. Although slightly exaggerated in parts, Kyle's description was more or less accurate. In a way, that only made things harder.

More than anything, Clint wanted to make sure the kids were safe and the best way to do that seemed to be in taking them to their aunt's place, wherever that might be. But, after talking to Jeremiah for just the little that he had and seeing the desperation in the man's eyes, Clint knew he had to do something to help him as well.

Thinking back to the rushed conversation, Clint recalled hearing that the man was being forced to do some kind of job against his will in order to protect his children. Whatever that job was, it couldn't have been good. Otherwise, the other men wouldn't have needed to use such drastic recruiting methods.

Clint had seen situations like this before. Whenever someone kidnapped another person, they would say or do whatever it took to get whatever they were after. And once they got whatever that was, they suddenly had no use for the hostage. In fact, that unlucky person was less of a hassle when they were dead—used up and tossed away like some piece of trash.

Besides that, Clint knew firsthand that those men down there were killers. They were ready and willing to blow away anyone that so much as inconvenienced them . . . even if that someone happened to be a pair of small children. Clint didn't have to know much more than that to figure that these men had killed before and would kill again as soon as it suited them. In fact, they might even decide to track down the eyes that had seen them kidnap the owner of the house they'd raided and put a bullet through each of the children just to keep them from talking to the law.

While Clint knew it didn't do anyone any good to get all riled up without having all the facts in front of him, he also knew that it would be a fatal mistake to underestimate a killer . . . let alone, an entire gang of them. And if that gang decided to tie up their loose ends by permanently silencing the children, Kyle and Sadie wouldn't be safe at their aunt's place. In fact, their aunt could very well join them in a shallow grave.

But that didn't mean they'd be any safer with him. Clint figured that going after the gang would be tricky enough without a pair of kids tagging along for the ride. One slip or cough at the wrong time and Clint might as well stand up and drop his pants for the shooters.

The more Clint thought about it, the more his head started to spin. So, rather than ponder the possibilities any further, he took the kids by their arms and pulled them farther up the ridge. "They're going to find that guard by the horses soon," he said. "I saw some of them head up that way. What I need you to do is stay put while I get my horse. And this time, I don't want you to say or throw *anything*."

"The trail loops around a little farther up in that direction," Kyle said while pointing to a spot behind Clint.

"Fine. I'll ride there and pick you up. And don't come out until you hear this." Clint whistled softly in a poor bird call.

Kyle nodded and took hold of his sister's hand. "Sure thing, mister."

At that moment, Sadie stepped up to Clint and looked up at him with hope brimming in her deep blue eyes. "Does this mean you're going to help us find Pa?"

Clint let out a deep breath. "Yeah. I guess it does."

TWENTY-FOUR

Of all the close calls he'd had in the last hour, Clint felt more tension when he made his way back to the spot where Eclipse was waiting as no fewer than half of the gunmen from the house started filing up the ridge. With all of those men staring closely at every rustling branch or any shifting leaf, this should have been the time for Clint to lay low and let the storm pass over him.

He knew the gunmen would find the one guard he'd tied up almost instantly. And if they caught sight of a strange horse anywhere near the area, they would know that the animal must belong to the one other person they'd spotted nearby.

Clint tried not to think about what might happen to Eclipse if he allowed the Darley Arabian to be found. The gunmen might decide to take the stallion for their own, leaving Clint with nothing but his own two feet to keep up with the killers. Or they might even decide to put a bullet into Eclipse just out of spite for its owner.

Either way they decided to go, Clint wasn't about to let it happen. And that was why, no matter how much his common sense told him to forget the idea for the immediate time being, he wound his way through the bushes amid a group of killers who already knew he was there. The only things in his advantage were the fact that all of the men were in unfamiliar territory and that the gunmen would probably be thinking that Clint wasn't stupid enough to attempt what he was in the middle of doing.

A bank of clouds was passing over the sun, giving Clint a bit more to work with by way of cover. Besides the bushes and leafy floor, he now had the newly arrived shadows to move within as he made his way carefully back to the spot where Eclipse was waiting. Not too long after he left the children, he found the place that Kyle had talked about where a part of the trail looped around nearby where he'd left the children. Clint stored that in the back of his mind and pressed on.

He quickly got used to blocking out the noises he made as he slithered through the dirt and leaves like some kind of overgrown snake. Soon, his ears were searching beyond the rustling of his own feet in the loose earth and became adept at picking out the noises that might possibly be coming from the men he was trying to avoid.

The first few noises he picked up that way were nothing but the passage of small animals who had much more purpose scurrying through the dirt than he did. He thought he'd heard a footstep nearby, but that turned out to be nothing more than something falling out of a nearby tree. But the third thing he heard was hard to confuse for anything so innocent.

This time, he heard what could only be a man walking along a path obscured by leaves and other debris. Clint froze in his spot, fully aware that he was not very well hidden at all. The only reason he'd been caught off guard was that he was moving through an area he thought to be far removed from the place where the horses were tied off. In fact, he'd been almost ready to get on his feet and walk for a ways until he got closer to what he considered to be a more dangerous area.

Clint pressed himself down against the ground until he could smell nothing but the soil and could feel nothing but the press of the earth against his flesh. His hands drifted reflexively toward the Colt at his side, preparing for the worst in case the approaching figure decided to look the wrong way at the wrong time.

All the while, he strained each of his senses to get a better idea of where, exactly, the person was coming from and how many of them there were. For a few seconds, he couldn't get anything but the footfalls crunching on dry leaves. But then a stray bit of movement caught his eye. It was just a branch flinching when it wasn't supposed to, but it was more than enough to warn him that someone was headed his way.

Clint lay on his belly with one hand stretched out in front of him and the other reaching down toward his holster. Despite the fact that he had a clump of bushes between himself and whoever was coming, he knew that wouldn't be enough to hide him completely. He was simply too big to disappear in this brush as effectively as the children who'd been doing it all their lives.

That was when he saw who'd been making all the noise. It was only two of the group of guards, but both of them had shotguns leveled in Clint's general direction. Their eyes scanned hastily from side to side, looking for their target while their fingers tensed anxiously upon their triggers.

Clint focused on them, even though he could just barely make out any details through the branches in front of him. Out of sheer necessity, however, he managed to spot the men's eyes, which were the key to knowing when he had to act or if he would even be spotted at all.

By the looks of them, the guards were instinctively looking straight ahead, figuring the man they were after would be crouched or even walking nearby. Although they weren't checking the ground just yet, Clint knew it was only a matter of seconds before they caught a glimpse of him lying no more than thirty feet away from them.

Both of Clint's hands clenched into fists.

His breath stayed in the back of his throat and he knew that even a slip as small as too loud of an exhale could bring him straight back into a firefight where the odds were stacked against him. Even though he could outdraw any of the men, the guards still had numbers on their side. Also, with the children waiting for him to return, Clint didn't exactly have the option of clearing a path and charging through it at the first opportunity.

Just as he closed his hand around the Colt, Clint thought once again about the children. That gave him an idea that almost seemed too easy to work. But then again, if it failed, he wouldn't be any worse off than he was at the moment.

Of course . . . there was also the possibility that a misguided action at this point could cost him his life. Clint preferred not to think about that part.

TWENTY-FIVE

Clint's fingers clamped shut and he lifted his arm just off the ground. But rather than draw the Colt, it was his left hand that moved, and that fist was closed around a small object that he launched into the air. The stone he'd picked up sailed noisily through a few branches before thumping onto the ground.

Both of the gunmen pivoted in that direction just as they were about to look at the spot where Clint was lying.

"What was that?" one of them whispered.

The second man turned away from Clint and pointed in the opposite direction. "I think I see him over there."

"Right. I know I heard something."

And with that, they moved off to investigate, giving Clint enough time to move past them and continue through the bushes until he was close enough to see the shapes of the horses shifting on their feet directly ahead.

The rest of the gunmen were making their way slowly up the path, searching for Clint as they walked. That gave him enough of an opportunity to take Eclipse's reins and climb into the saddle. Clint could already hear the gunmen approaching the rest of the horses, which were tied up a little farther down the trail. Without wasting the time to look back, Clint snapped the reins and steered the Darley Arabian stallion back the way he'd originally come.

This time, rather than stick to the main path, he veered off on the offshoot that would loop him back to where the children should be waiting for him. If he hadn't known exactly where this detour was, he never would have found it since it was all but completely covered by fallen leaves and branches that had grown in over the years.

He pushed Eclipse as fast as he could manage given the tricky terrain. And when he got close to the agreed spot, he gave out the call and prayed the kids hadn't gone off on their own again.

Just as he was about to whistle again, Clint spotted some movement nearby. First, all he could see was the shifting of some branches. Then, a small face appeared, followed by another. Both of those faces lit up the instant they spotted him and soon Kyle and Sadie were rushing out into the open.

"Hurry up now," Clint said while leaning down in the saddle and offering his hand to Kyle. "We've got to get out of here while the getting's good."

Kyle took Clint's hand and hopped up just as Clint hoisted him into the saddle behind him.

"Did you steal one of their horses?" the boy asked with wide-eyed admiration.

Making sure Kyle was secure on the stallion's back and not about to slide off when they took off, Clint replied, "No. This is Eclipse. He's rightfully mine." And when he felt Kyle's arms lock around his midsection, Clint reached down to grab hold of Sadie, who was already jumping up and down next to the Darley Arabian.

She smiled widely when she finally was lifted off her feet and placed between Clint and the saddle horn. "Hello, Eclipse," she said while cinching herself in. "You're beautiful."

Clint held onto both reins with one hand and looped

the other around Sadie before touching his heels to Eclipse's sides. Already, he could hear the sounds of the other horses being led off by the gunmen. And judging by the angry shouting and swearing, the first guard he'd tied up had also been found as well. "You two better hang on," he said. "We've got to get out of here real quick."

Both Kyle and Sadie appeared completely at ease while riding. Even when Eclipse had to jump over a fallen log or a hole in the trail, neither one of the children seemed even close to falling from the saddle. The stallion seemed to sense Clint's anxiousness and put as much distance as he could between itself and Jeremiah's house as quickly as his four legs would allow.

Clint's senses were still on the alert for any trace of the gunmen. He'd been fully expecting them to be hot on his trail, but the sounds of their footsteps seemed to fade away twice as fast as he might have hoped for. Not until they'd gotten clear of the thick bushes did Clint take a moment to pull back on the reins and allow Eclipse to catch his breath.

Bringing the stallion around so he could get a clear look behind him, Clint saw that there wasn't even one gunman coming up from that direction. He figured that the ones he'd heard had only been a handful of the total number sent to fetch the horses, but that didn't mean that he would allow himself to relax just yet.

In fact, the moment he thought along those lines, he heard the sound of hooves beating upon the ground. Rather than wait to see how many had decided to come after him and the children, Clint turned Eclipse away from the house once again, gave a word of warning to the kids and set Eclipse into a full gallop.

The stallion's head moved back and forth, his breath huffing in powerful bursts similar to those that came from a steam engine. Even with all the trouble surrounding them, Clint couldn't help but enjoy the feel of raw power emitting from the Darley Arabian's powerful mass. Looking down, Clint saw that he wasn't the only one savoring the moment, as a wide, gleeful smile adorned Sadie's face.

Sadie looked up at him, smiled just a bit wider and then hunkered down over Eclipse's neck. Not wanting to tempt fate any more than he already had, Clint kept up the pace until they were able to lose themselves in a series of twists and turns that led them up along the slope of another nearby hill. With Kyle's help, he managed to find a few narrow paths that eventually ended at a shelf of rock overlooking the way they'd come.

Clint wasn't too familiar with the area, but he knew they'd be awful hard to find unless the gunmen were right on their tail. And though the sound of their horses thundered in the background, the others were still too far behind to have followed them all the way.

A few minutes passed before Clint caught sight of the gunmen. They were heading east on a trail that took them away from where he and the children had gone. Using the spyglass, Clint was able to get a look at the group of killers.

"Where are they going?" Kyle asked from his seat on the back of the saddle.

Clint squinted through the lenses and shook his head. "I don't know for sure. Looks like they're not coming after us, though."

Pressing her back against Clint for support, Sadie lowered her head and asked, "Are you sure?"

"Yeah," Clint answered. "Pretty sure. If they'd have wanted us, they could've come after us a little harder or even tracked us down. We weren't exactly covering our trail."

"Good," she said, her muscles relaxing somewhat. "They were bad men."

Clint nodded in agreement, but kept his telescope trained on the line of horses in the distance.

"Is my pa with them?" Kyle asked.

Having just spotted what he thought to be the man he'd talked to after charging out of the house, Clint hesitated for a moment before answering. "Yeah," he said finally. "I think he is."

The boy shifted and squirmed on Eclipse's back. "What do we do now?"

Clint thought about the string of events that had taken him from a comfortable ride to dodging bullets, and winding up with him acting as custodian for two small children. Having already weighed his options, Clint still felt the pressure of his decision and no matter how much he didn't like it, there was only one choice available. "We do the only thing we can," he said to himself as well as to his passengers. "We go after your father."

TWENTY-SIX

The ride over the border into Kentucky was quick and easy. Brody knew exactly where he was going and despite all the troubles his men were expecting, their prisoner didn't put up much of a struggle at all. In fact, Jeremiah even started bantering with some of the men and was even getting along with Brody himself. It was almost as if they'd taken in a new member of the gang.

For his part, Brody enjoyed the painless passage to Haddleville, but he made it perfectly clear that his guard was never down. He posted scouts every night and rode in strict formation every day, always preparing for trouble no matter how little indication he had that such precautions were necessary.

And behind the killers, Clint and the two children were never far off. They stuck to the rougher terrain, but only so far as they needed to go for ample cover. There were always woodlands or higher trails to be taken and Clint kept to those in order to stay out of harm's way. He was always ready to send Eclipse and the children into thicker trees or the occasional cavern if Brody's men got too close, but that never proved necessary.

Instead, the gunmen appeared to be on a tight schedule

and as long as they didn't catch sight nor sound of Clint, they seemed more than happy to move along toward wherever they were going. It became obvious after a few days that they were headed in a specific direction and now that they were almost there, Clint thought he knew what that direction was.

Currently, he and the children were taking a rest so they could stretch their legs and take in some of the rations from Clint's saddlebags. They were more in the open than what they'd become used to and this fact was quickly discovered by Kyle, who walked up to Clint with his thumbs hooked through the belt loops of his pants.

"How come we're not up there?" the boy asked, pointing to a patch of trees less than a quarter mile away. "Shouldn't we be in there in case they're lookin' for us?"

"Don't worry," Clint said. "They're not looking for us. Not right now, anyway." In the short amount of time he'd known them, Clint had become accustomed to talking to both children. In fact, he was actually starting to enjoy the conversations that took up most of their time. "They've been keeping their distance from every town we passed, but we're coming up on one soon and they seem to be steering straight for it."

"Really?" Sadie asked, suddenly appearing next to him as if from nowhere. "Is that where they're taking Poppa?"

"That's what it looks like. We'll follow them in to be sure, but I've got a feeling that's where they've been headed this whole time."

"Why?" Kyle asked. "What town is that?"

Clint turned to face the boy and knelt down to his level. "It's called Haddleville. Ever hear of it?"

Kyle shook his head.

"Not even from your father?"

Taking a moment to wrinkle the corners of his eyes in concentration, Kyle pondered that for a few seconds and then shrugged. "Nope," he said with another shake of his head.

Having done more than his fair share of gambling over the years, Clint had heard plenty about Haddleville. Mostly, the things he heard were from other gamblers who'd passed through the place when it was known as a money town. Several places had held that same title, but usually didn't keep it for more than a few months. Gamblers called any place that seemed to be hosting the biggest games and doling out the best payouts a money town.

Haddleville had held this distinction almost as many times as places such as Dodge City or Leadville. But what also made that town stick in Clint's mind was something else a little more noteworthy than it having an occasional streak of good luck. And it was that particular something that made Clint think about who Kyle's father was and what those gunmen might have wanted from him.

"What did you say your father's name was?"

Kyle stood up tall and spoke proudly. "Jeremiah Garver."

Taking in the name and rolling it around in his head for a moment or two, Clint searched his brain for any hint of recognition. But there was nothing he could put his finger on that made that name stand out from any other. "And can you tell me some more about him? Any stories he might have told you about things he'd done or where he'd been?"

Kyle suddenly seemed to shrink away from Clint. He lowered his eyes and took a step back, his posture drooping slightly like a reed bending in the wind. ". . . No. I . . . I can't think of anything like that."

"That's not true!" Sadie piped up. "You told me that Poppa was quick with a pistol and rode the trail with—"

Kyle reached over and swatted his sister on the side of the head. "Shut up, Sadie!"

TWENTY-SEVEN

Taking the boy by the shoulders, Clint looked Kyle straight in the eyes and said, "It's all right, Kyle. You can trust me. I only want to know so I can help him and you and your sister." He made sure to keep his voice calm and as even as possible figuring that, although Sadie might be more willing to talk to him, Kyle was his best bet for getting accurate information.

Staring down at his feet while kicking at the dirt beneath them, Kyle started to talk a couple of times, but stopped himself before any words came out. Finally, he looked up and said, "Pa told me he used to . . . used to ride with bad men."

Hearing that, Sadie's eyes widened as though she was listening to a tale of adventure and exciting battles.

"He caught me stealing one time from the general store," Kyle went on. "It was just a piece of candy, but he made me take it back and when he punished me, he said that he used to steal too and that no good could come from it."

"What did he used to steal?" Clint asked.

Kyle shrugged. "He said he used to be a bad man before he met Ma, but he was trying to be better now that

107

she was gone and that me and Sadie should honor her memory by being good people. He said he didn't want me to be like him when I grew up."

"I wanna be like him!" Sadie chirped. "I wanna ride a horse like Eclipse and shoot a gun!"

Although Clint was far from knowing all about Jeremiah Garver, he was getting a much clearer picture of the man. And what he'd heard seemed to fit perfectly with the man he'd spoken to outside of the house right before he'd managed to make his escape. Jeremiah had seemed frightened, but not for himself. And the gunmen seemed hell-bent on taking Jeremiah with them . . . no matter what they had to do to accomplish the task.

Clint could even feel the temptation to scold Sadie for what she'd said about taking up a gun, but he knew the girl was only playing and had no real notion about the life she was asking for. Turning his attention back to Kyle, he said, "Your pa knew those men who came for him. Did you know about that?"

Kyle's eyes became wide and his skin grew pale. "No, sir."

"Haddleville has a lot of money in its bank that lots of bad men know about. Did he tell you anything about that when he told you about what he used to do before meeting your mother?"

That did seem to spark something within the boy. "He talked to Pete King in town about the bank in Stony Trail once. Pa told him that anyone with half a mind could bust open that safe and ride off without a scratch. I don't think he meant for me to hear that, though."

Clint nodded as the picture of Jeremiah Garver became even more focused in his brain. Apparently, the man had some knowledge of banks, and if those gunmen wanted him so badly, that meant he must be a specialist of some kind.

"Did I help you any?" Kyle asked.

"You sure did," Clint answered. "In fact, if you were older, I'd say I owed you a drink for all the help you've given me so far."

"What about me?" Sadie asked.

Clint reached down and picked the little girl up. She smiled broadly as she was lifted into the air and set down in her familiar spot in Eclipse's saddle. "You too," he said. "I owe both of you a drink, but it'll have to wait until we get back with your father. Does that sound all right?"

Sadie leaned forward to dig both hands into Eclipse's mane, scratching the stallion's neck vigorously. "I guess."

Climbing into the saddle, Clint reached a hand down for Kyle. "Ready to head into town where we can get ourselves a real meal and a nice bed to sleep in?"

That was more than enough to brighten both of their moods. Even Clint found that he was looking forward to getting some walls around himself and the children rather than having them all sleep in the open so close to a gang of killers.

They rode into Haddleville at a leisurely pace. Clint was doing so to make sure the gang was far enough ahead that they didn't look back at the wrong time and spot them trailing behind the bigger group. Playing the part of unwelcome shadow to a bunch of gunmen was never a good idea, even in the best of circumstances. But with two children in tow, Clint had to be extra careful. He didn't even want to think about what it would feel like to see Kyle or Sadie catch a stray bullet.

They all made idle conversation as they rode and Clint kept a watchful eye on the trail ahead. It didn't take long for him to lose sight of the gunmen completely, since they took off in a rush once they got close to Haddleville's limits. Seeing that, Clint felt certain he knew what they were going after.

A man didn't have to be an outlaw to know the stories

about the vault at the First Bank of Haddleville. Just being
in their midst was enough to pick up rumors of shipments
ranging in the tens of thousands of dollars floating in and
out of that bank with a good amount of frequency. And
there were plenty of lawmen around to not only pass
along those stories, but verify them as well.

It was enough to make an honest man consider the prudence of his morals. Especially when hitting one bank
would be enough to make him a rich man for the rest of
his life. The tales of Haddleville's vault ranked up with
modern legend and if they were even half true, they were
definitely worth any robber's time.

Clint knew that if Jeremiah Garver was a specialist in
bank robberies, then that could only mean the gang had
abducted him for a purpose. And in Haddleville, there was
only one purpose on a thief's mind.

The moment they rode into town, Clint took the children to a small, yet clean boardinghouse with comfortable
beds and the smell of good food drifting up from the
kitchen. He also made sure that it was as far from the
bank as he could possibly manage.

TWENTY-EIGHT

"You haven't said much since we got here," Brody said to the man who rode on the horse next to him.

Jeremiah stared straight ahead, much the same as he'd been doing ever since he'd left his home a few days ago. Although he'd been doing his level best to try and get in good with the rest of the gang, his mind had been anywhere but with them as they rode into Kentucky. Even as they came into Haddleville, Jeremiah felt as though his heart was still wandering through the brush surrounding his house, searching for the children he envisioned huddled there alone and scared.

Brody looked back at the rest of his men. Most of them were exchanging loaded glances between one another and none of them seemed too concerned with the man they'd all but stopped considering a prisoner. Marcus, on the other hand, kept a few paces behind Jeremiah. He'd held position there throughout the entire trip and seemed ready to draw on Jeremiah as soon as he deemed it appropriate.

Brody took some comfort from the other man's paranoia. In fact, he wouldn't have had it any other way.

"I suppose we'll run this the way we ran all our other jobs," Jeremiah said.

"This ain't exactly like any of our other jobs," Brody pointed out. "In fact, this might very well be the *last* job."

Jeremiah's shoulders shook up and down and he let out a grumbling laugh. "I've heard that song before. Let's see, the last time was in Cheyenne when we knocked over that bank and stagecoach in the same day. That one was supposed to set us up for life."

Brody chuckled too, except his laughter had more of a steely edge beneath the surface. "That would have set us up if we weren't working with a bunch of greedy bastards who couldn't keep their heads down for a few months afterward. If we hadn't get caught—"

"But we didn't get caught. Those greedy bastards did."

"Sure . . . but they also took most of the money." Brody nodded and let the memories flow through him. "We had some good times, didn't we?"

"No," Jeremiah said without a moment's hesitation. "You had all the good times. I was just along to do my job and make my money."

"Don't give me that. I saw the look in your eyes during them jobs. Part of the reason I came back for you was to give you that look in your eyes one more time."

"I've heard *this* song too," Jeremiah interrupted. "And you can save it because I don't feel like listening to it again."

"All right, all right. That's the last time I try to change your life around to something worth living. Will you at least consider joining me on a regular basis? Maybe as one of my partners that I don't have to kidnap?"

Jeremiah's first instinct was to react with the disgust that churned in his belly at the way he was playing up to Brody. But he knew that if he didn't put the gang's leader at ease, he would quickly lose what little slack the gunmen had been giving him. As it was, he knew he was already on thin ice when it came to Marcus.

"I'll think about it after we're done here," Jeremiah

said, while managing to choke back the bile that rose up in the back of his throat. As much as it disgusted him, he put a friendly smile on his face for the sake of the children. After all, he wouldn't be any good to them if he wound up dead from looking cross-eyed at the wrong man.

"You do that," Brody said with a wink. "And in the meantime, I've got someone to see in regards to the little withdrawal we're planning on making. Why don't you ride along with the rest of the boys and put up the horses. I'll catch up with you tonight and we can talk some more over drinks. Catch up on old times."

Jeremiah didn't mistake the amiable tone in Brody's voice for true friendliness. The gang's leader was giving him an order, plain and simple. If he wanted to test that theory, all Jeremiah had to do was refuse to do the simple task he'd been given. But he'd already made that mistake the first time he and Brody had ridden together. The result was one of the uglier scars on Jeremiah's neck when Brody had almost sliced his throat open. "Sure, Brody. I'll lend a hand."

Brody watched as all but one of his men turned off on another street and rode away. Remaining at his side, Marcus kept his eye on Jeremiah's back as though he half expected the man to turn on them both with guns blazing.

"I don't trust him," Marcus said once the rest of the gang had ridden out of sight around a corner.

Brody let his friendly manner boil away like wax dripping away from the rest of the candle. "And you think I do?"

"Then why do you talk to him like that? I swear you're trying to get him in the gang when he ain't nothin' but a run-down farmer anymore. He may have been somethin' years ago, but them days is past."

"He's got a few good days in him. And I plan on using them all up while we're here."

For one of the rare times since Brody had known him, Marcus started to smile. "And how's he leavin' town?"

"Feet first."

"That's the best news I heard all day."

Both men snapped their reins and headed off toward the busier section of town. The streets of Haddleville were busy enough at any time of day that the outlaws didn't have to worry about sticking out of the crowd enough to be noticed. The people passing them by were a diverse mix of locals, cowboys, gamblers, and even a lot more unsavory-looking characters than the worst of Brody's men.

"You know something?" Marcus said. "I kind of like it here."

"I was just thinking the same thing. It'll be a shame to burn it down."

That notion brought a smile to both of the men's faces, which lasted all the way until they got to their destination. The Mason Dixon Hotel loomed over them like an estate home planted in the middle of the bustling street. Brody and Marcus tied their horses to a post outside and stepped into the finely decorated lobby.

TWENTY-NINE

Haddleville was a big town. Clint had heard plenty about how much the place had grown, but was still surprised by just how busy it was. There were plenty of towns with more space within their limits or buildings on their blocks, but Haddleville made the best of every inch it had. From the saloons to the gambling halls to the hotels built to fill them all, every location in town was bumping right up against the next and its streets wound between them in a tangle of dirt and boardwalks.

After settling the account for the rented room under an assumed name, Clint was confident that Mrs. Brasser, the older woman who ran the boardinghouse he'd chosen, would take care of the children just fine. In fact, she seemed thrilled at the prospect of keeping an eye on them from time to time.

Clint hated leaving them out of his sight so close to the other gunmen, but he knew that Kyle wasn't about to let his sister wander out of the boardinghouse for any reason whatsoever. After meeting with Mrs. Brasser, Sadie was excited to learn to bake from the older lady, who'd raised no fewer than nine of her own children.

As Clint left the boardinghouse, he felt a pang of uncertainty about letting the kids out of his sight. But that disappeared the moment he thought about the reason they were there in the first place. He had a man to find and killers to stop, which was most definitely not a place for children. Besides, they seemed to handle themselves well enough when their own home had been under siege. Sitting in a boardinghouse for a while would be a cakewalk in comparison.

The last time he'd been in Haddleville, Clint had rarely left his poker table for much longer than the time it took to rest and take in a meal. Although some of it seemed vaguely familiar, he knew he wouldn't feel as though he'd actually been there before unless he stepped into the Inside Straight Poker Palace on Third Street.

This time, Clint was in town for much more than a few hands of cards. Rather than stroll along and take in the atmosphere, his eyes were focusing on every face he passed, searching every doorway and each alleyway for a trace of one of the killers he'd seen. What sat like a rock in the pit of his stomach was the fact that he hadn't gotten a good look at even half of the gunmen. He could very well have walked right past a few of them and looked them in the eyes without being much the wiser. And once one of them recognized him, the deadly game would be taken quickly to the next level.

With this in mind, Clint kept his chin down and the brim of his hat over his eyes as much as possible without getting in the way of his search. He knew from watching the gunmen before that they were a precise team that functioned well together. Prudence told him not to judge the killers by the fact that the children had gotten away from them. And the more he thought about that, the more Clint became of the mind that they'd let the kids go once their father had agreed to go along quietly.

Clint shook his head at the guts it took for Jeremiah to hand himself over like that. Being a man who knew well enough how the killers' minds worked, he couldn't have been stupid enough to think that they'd simply let him go once the job was done. That man knew he could very well be signing his own death warrant, which made Clint resolve himself even more to the task of saving his life.

He'd walked almost halfway through town by now and still had yet to see a familiar face. Some of the street corners and storefronts were jogging his memory, but that didn't do him a lot of good at the moment. He turned down Second Avenue and looked all the way down to where the road dead-ended almost two blocks away. Standing there like a wooden monument to finance was the First Bank of Haddleville.

The building itself was two floors high and only slightly smaller than the town hall. Its foundation was constructed out of brick, giving the impression that the bank was rooted in solid rock. Even the wooden walls seemed thick and imposing, which made the structure look almost like a fortress, complete with the row of flags waving in the breeze along the edge of the roof.

With the bank in sight, Clint felt a nervous chill run through his bones. He knew that on a normal day this place was being watched by predators who circled the imposing structure as though they could smell a fresh kill. Besides the outlaws who viewed the bank as the job of a lifetime, there were also lawmen and guards patrolling the bank's perimeter with guns in open view.

Some had shotguns cradled in their arms and others had rifles hefted over their shoulders. All of them wore holsters around their waists with one or two pistols for each man. Even from a block away, Clint could see the armaments on display, which was the point of having the guards walking around the building in the first place. They were there on display as well as to protect. Form and function all wrapped up in one.

Clint stopped for a second to take in the impressive

sight once he was close enough to see it all. Second Avenue came to a stop on Cottonwood, which was where the bank had been built. Standing at the intersection, Clint looked at the bank, its guards, its walls, and all the well-dressed customers who walked in and out of its doors, wearing their money on their backs in the form of silk suits, diamond tie tacks, and gold chains crossing their bellies.

Impressed, Clint shook his head and said softly to himself, "Jesus. Even I'm thinking about robbing this place."

And almost as though they'd sensed the notions swirling in Clint's head, two of Brody's men walked past him as though they were out for nothing but a stroll. Clint recognized them as two of the guards he'd knocked out at Jeremiah's house and had no doubt that they would recognize him just as quickly if they turned around at the wrong time. Before that could happen, Clint lowered his hat and stepped back casually after they'd passed.

He kept an eye on them just in case they'd already spotted him and were about to try and take him by surprise. Once the guards were far enough away, Clint scanned the area around him and found nothing suspicious in the crowd. There wasn't a single eye trained on him for too long or one hand moving too close to a weapon.

Not foolish enough to think he was completely safe, Clint moved away from Cottonwood Street and headed for a nearby saloon with a view of the bank. Something was going to happen soon, he knew. And when it did, the explosion would be felt throughout the entire town.

THIRTY

The Mason Dixon Hotel might have been several blocks away from the bank in Haddleville, but Brody still felt as though he could reach out and touch the vault he'd come to break. He took in a deep breath, smelling the fear he would cause and the money he would take every bit as much as he could pick out the scents of cooking food and cigar smoke. All of those smells wafted throughout the lobby and were even more powerful inside the hotel's gambling hall.

"I swear, Marcus," Brody said while glancing over to the man standing beside him. "If we didn't have to pull a job here, I'd want to settle down in this place."

Marcus laughed once under his breath. "If you didn't have to pull a job here, you'd think this place was too loud and packed full of too many people."

"You're probably right. Maybe I should keep that in mind when I'm ready to settle someplace."

"That would go over just fine. Get a nice little house somewhere, find a wife, and spend your days planning to knock a hole in the bank or rob the train that passes through every Friday."

Brody scowled slightly. "If I didn't know any better,

I'd say you were having a joke at my expense."

"Actually, I am having a rather large joke at your expense. The thought of any of us settling somewhere should be enough to give anyone a healthy laugh."

"It worked for Jeremiah."

Hearing that name was all it took to put a mean glare on Marcus's face. "We'll see how well it works for him when I empty that pathetic jackass's stomach onto the floor of that bank. He can do all his settling in a hole outside of town."

"I won't hear that kind of talk about a member of my gang," Brody said sternly. "At least, not until he's finished with the job I hired him for."

Marcus shook his head and looked around the room. Even in the late afternoon, the Mason Dixon's card tables were nearly full. The card players there were the kind who would be sitting in the same spots all day long, as well as all night long and well into the next few days. Fortunes changed hands in rooms like those, not all of which happened over poker hands.

"Who are we supposed to meet here?" Marcus asked.

"A friend of mine who's been our eyes and ears inside that bank for the last month or so." Pausing for a few seconds, Brody fixed his eyes on a table in the middle of the room. "Ah . . . I see they still know how to keep an appointment."

Looking in the same direction as Brody, Marcus quickly found one of the few tables in the room that wasn't covered with poker chips and half-empty glasses. Sitting there was a pair of smartly dressed men who kept their backs straight and their noses turned up in the air. Next to one of them was a busty redhead wearing a crushed velvet dress with a neckline cut low enough to display her impressively ample curves.

"Now remember, Marcus," Brody said as he started working his way between the tables and gamblers. "Try to keep your language clean and your temper in check. We don't want to scare away our pigeons before they hand over the keys to the coop."

Once they were close enough to the table to attract the attention of everyone sitting there, Brody and Marcus removed their hats and took a seat. Almost before their backsides could make a dent in the cushions, a server rushed over to them and took drink orders.

"Nothing too strong for me," Brody said. "I'll just have water."

"Same here," Marcus replied when the server glanced down at him.

The man sitting beside the redhead nodded approvingly. "Are you quite sure? They have an impeccably stocked bar. I can recommend a red wine that I'm sure you'd find—"

Brody held up his hand and said, "Not just now. We've got business to discuss."

The others nodded in agreement and the server took that as his cue to leave. Once he was gone, everyone at the table still waited for a second or two just to make sure that the outsider was out of earshot. Brody was the first one to clear his throat and set things into motion.

"This is Marcus Abels, a trusted partner of mine," Brody said while nodding toward the chair next to him.

The man sitting beside the redhead extended his hand and greeted Marcus formally. "Pleased to meet you. I'm Sherman Pierce. I've done business with Mr. Brody for some time. And this lovely lady next to me is Nicole Walsh. Don't worry, she won't try to impede the proceedings."

Smiling vacantly, Nicki offered her hand to Marcus and smiled warmly when he took it. She then turned to Brody and did the same. Only when she looked at him, Nicki held his gaze slightly longer than a casual greeting would dictate. "Nice to see you again."

Brody took her hand and then looked over to the man next to Pierce. "And I don't believe I know you, Mr. . . ."

"Altwell," the man next to Pierce said in a gruff voice. He appeared to be in his late fifties and wore his chin whiskers in a thick tuft beneath a severely downturned mouth. Of all the people sitting at the table, Altwell was dressed the most like a rich businessman. His black suit almost resembled the style preferred by many of the gamblers, except for the fact that it looked to be of a finer cut and there was no bulge beneath either of his arms.

"Good to meet you and all of that," Brody said, his voice edged with impatience. "But the matters I'd like to discuss are of a . . . private nature."

"Oh, don't worry about that," Pierce intoned. "Mr. Altwell has been involved in some very prestigious—"

"Good for him," Brody interrupted. When he spoke, he looked directly at Pierce and seemed to ignore the fact that Altwell was even among the rest of them. "That's just great. But my business is none of his. I'd appreciate it if you would ask him to leave."

Pierce seemed genuinely confused. "But I'm sure that—"

"Leave," Marcus said. "Now."

THIRTY-ONE

Clearing his throat as though he was trying to chastise one of his grandchildren, Altwell pushed away from the table and stood up. "Perfectly fine," he said. "I wouldn't dream of poking my nose in if I'm not wanted."

Although Brody looked up at the older man, he still didn't see fit to say a word to him. Instead, he simply fixed his eyes on Altwell and didn't take them away until the other man turned on his heels and strode away.

Pierce seemed more than a little uncomfortable with the affair and took a sip of his drink. He stared down at his glass even though it was empty and cleared his throat once Altwell had disappeared into the crowd. "Sorry about that," he said. "But I thought you might benefit from his ideas."

"Nice thought," Brody replied. "But I prefer to deal specifically with you." Leaning over the table a bit, he reached out and slapped Pierce on the shoulder. "That's just one less way to split the profits, eh?"

That struck Pierce as exceptionally funny and it also seemed to take away some of the tension that had been hanging in the air. Once the laughter died down, Pierce took a deep breath and set both elbows onto the table.

"Are the rest of your partners in town yet?"

"No," Brody lied without so much as a twitch to give him away. "But they'll be along. Is everything set on this end?"

"Actually, there's been a slight delay." When he saw the shadow pass over Brody's face, Pierce quickly went on to set it right. "But not a big one. Just a day or so. Carrying out transactions of the size we're planning will require the bank to have more capital on hand. I thought it would be ready tomorrow, but it should actually be set up for the next day. I hope that's not too much of an inconvenience."

Brody nodded subtly and looked over to Marcus. "No, that should be fine. And will the bank be able to fulfill our needs?"

"There's going to be two major payrolls coming in along with some railroad deposits that should be more than enough to carry out the transactions we'd planned."

"Excellent." Looking over to Marcus, Brody couldn't help but be amused by the poorly hidden confusion written all over the other man's face. "Do you have any questions?" he asked the gunman.

Marcus looked at Brody and then at Pierce. Having sat in on plenty of meetings before going on a job, Marcus was used to double-talk and code when they were in public. But this was something that threw him for a loop. "I wouldn't even know where to begin," he said while shaking his head.

Brody truly enjoyed the look on his partner's face and kept right on enjoying it for the next hour or two as all four of them had drinks and talked about business. All the while, Nicki kept her eyes roaming between Brody and Marcus. She laughed at all the right jokes and smiled whenever she was being addressed.

And no matter how many times he requested to talk to Brody alone, Marcus was never able to tear the other man away from the table. It was as though Brody found all the talk about business futures and accounting to be suddenly more fascinating than anything else the town had to offer, including the bank that they'd come to rob.

Unable to hide his frustration any longer, Marcus excused himself and pushed away from the table.

"Where are you going?" Brody asked.

"To the bar. I think I need another drink. Should I get you anything?"

"No. I'll be staying on for a bit and then we'll have a private meeting before wrapping up for the day." Even though he was dressed in the clothes he'd been wearing on the trail and was wearing a gun that had ended countless lives, Brody conducted himself like one of Pierce's most upstanding confidants.

Shaking his head and letting out an exasperated breath, Marcus turned his back on the group and headed for the bar.

Watching the other man go, Pierce cocked his head slightly and looked back to Brody. "Is he all right?"

Brody waved off the question as though it had been buzzing noisily around his head. "He's a bit tired. Besides, he never had a mind for business like you and I."

That was more than enough of a stroke to Pierce's ego to satisfy the well-dressed businessman. "I didn't bring the rest of my papers since I thought Altwell would keep us busy for most of the evening. If you'd like, I can get them and we can continue this later. I take it you'd prefer the rest of the meeting to be in private?"

"Yes," Brody said, while looking away from Pierce. "I would definitely enjoy that."

THIRTY-TWO

Brody sat at the table alone for a few minutes after Pierce and his companion had gone. When he finally got up, he noticed Marcus standing at the bar on the other end of the room. Knowing that the gunman would do just fine on his own, Brody walked out of the gambling area, through the lobby and out the front door.

Although it wasn't even five o'clock yet, the sun was on its way down and the sky was turning the bright, fiery color of the early dusk of autumn. Brody always preferred this time of year when darkness came so much earlier than in the summer. It gave him more time to steal and thicker shadows from which to strike. And when he thought of that, he spotted one shadow in particular that caught his interest.

Brody fished in his shirt pocket for a cigarette he'd rolled while talking to Pierce and walked across the street. The shadow he'd seen was in the doorway of a saloon opposite from the Mason Dixon Hotel and was starting to move just as Brody got close enough to reach out and touch it.

"I think your friend was expecting something a little different," came a voice from the darkness.

Brody smiled and reached out to place his hand on the wall next to the doorway. "Marcus didn't know what to expect because I didn't tell him. It's so rare that I get to see that perplexed look on his face that I simply couldn't resist."

The shadow shifted somewhat as the person waiting inside it stepped forward. Nicki moved out to press herself so close to Brody that he could feel the touch of her breasts against his chest.

"Have you been keeping an eye on our Mr. Pierce?" Brody asked.

"Of course I have. But I've been waiting for you to come back so long that it started to hurt." Nicki took hold of one of Brody's wrists and pulled his hand to her. Placing his palm on her chest, she lowered her voice to a seductive purr. "It hurt right here. And I feel so empty," she said, sliding his hand down below her waist, "right here."

Even though Brody's body was responding to the feel of the warmth beneath Nicki's dress, he somehow managed to keep his mind from wandering too far from its original course. "And what about when you weren't playing nursemaid to the vice president of my favorite bank? Have you been keeping up with the rest of your duties?"

Nicki's eyes were closed and she rubbed herself against Brody's palm. "Mmm. Yes," she whispered. "I got a good look at the inside of the bank just like you asked. And I even know how many guards are on patrol during every shift of the day."

Brody smiled at that, moving his fingers on the hand that she held as if he was gently strumming the strings of a guitar. "Very good. And what else do you have for me?"

Pouting slightly in frustration, Nicki ground her hips against Brody in an attempt to distract him from his question. But even though she could feel the hardness between his legs, she couldn't get him to respond fully the way she so desperately wanted . . . the way she needed. Finally, she said, "I can tell you anything you want about that place. And Pierce doesn't know a thing about you."

Pushing his hips forward just enough to rub his groin against Nicki's, Brody smiled even wider. "Ahhh, that's better."

Nicki's eyes widened and she pulled in a quick gasp of air. When she felt his thick shaft through his pants as well as through the folds of her dress, she wrapped her arms around him and gyrated against him in a way that brushed his erect member against the sweet spot between her legs. "He doesn't know anything about why you're really here. And he still doesn't suspect anything. You can do what you want." Moving her gaze up from his waist, over his chest, and then locking onto his eyes, she added, "Anything you want. However many times you want."

Maintaining his passive facade was becoming harder and harder for Brody as his own desires started burning through. The bank was slipping away toward the back of his mind and the details of the upcoming robbery were becoming nothing more than distractions from what he wanted to do more than anything else in the world. His hands started moving on their own, exploring her body as though they were already alone together rather than sharing the semi-seclusion of a shadow of a darkened doorway.

Although folks in Haddleville, like those in any other large town, knew to keep to their own affairs, it was hard for them not to notice the couple standing out in the open, pawing hungrily at each other's bodies. The only thing that saved them from becoming a true spectacle was the fact that most of the locals recognized Nicki either in face or figure and weren't surprised in the least to see her entwined with a strange man. When they caught sight of her striking red hair or full, expressive lips, they simply grinned to themselves and kept walking. Most of the ones who saw didn't bother looking at Brody. After all, he wasn't half as pleasing to the eye as the woman accompanying him.

"You haven't lost your touch, have you?" Brody whispered as he came somewhat back to his senses.

Her lips parted in a smile that betrayed every dirty notion that was coursing through her mind. "Maybe I should remind you just how good my touch is. And if you don't ask me to take you back to my room soon, I'll have to remind you right here."

Brody was about to continue the game by prolonging the agony just a little more, but he suddenly felt her fingers stroking his rigid penis through his clothing and knew he couldn't bring himself to wait any longer. "All right," he said. "But all I can say is that your room better be damn close."

Nicki gave him one more gentle squeeze before moving her hand to his and taking him by the wrist. Victorious in the contest of wills, she led him away from the saloon and down the boardwalk, keeping her steps purposefully slower than Brody found comfortable. "Have you been thinking about me since you've been away?" she asked.

"Every night."

"Do you remember the night we spent the last time you were here? How you tore off every stitch of clothing from my body and licked me from head to toe?"

Brody let out a sound from the back of his throat that was part affirmation and part snarl.

Hearing that, Nicki turned to look at him over her shoulder while licking her lips. "And do you remember how I would brush my hair over your chest and how you used to play with it when I had you in my mouth? When you held me there and wouldn't let me climb on top of you, it made me wetter than I've ever been. Do you remember that?"

This time, Brody didn't even make a sound. All he could do was glare at her with a desire that burned in his belly with so much intensity that it threatened to consume him. Not only could he remember what she was talking about, but he could also remember the way her skin felt beneath his fingertips and the way her juices tasted in his mouth.

Leading Brody by the hand as well as by other things, Nicki turned away from him to look and make sure she was headed in the right direction to take him to her room. But the instant she turned her back on him, she suddenly couldn't move another inch. She might have tripped at the abrupt stop, but Brody was right there to catch her.

"I remember all of that," he said in a fierce whisper. "And now it's all I can think about."

Nicki felt her heart start to pound inside her chest and said, "Good. Then come along with me and we can relive some of those memories."

"No," Brody hissed, tugging her in another direction completely. "I can't wait that long. I want to make some new memories right now."

And before she could respond at all, Nicki was pulled a little farther down the street toward a dark storefront that was just out of the line of sight for those people walking to and from the nearby hotel.

THIRTY-THREE

Brody didn't take the time to look and see what kind of store it was. All he knew was that it seemed dark and empty and that the door was locked when he first tried to pull it open. He solved the latter problem with a swift kick that sent the flimsy door swinging inward to pound against the inside wall.

Feeling his hands lock around her upper arms to keep her from moving away from him and seeing the way he was ready to knock down anything that kept him from her a moment longer, Nicki became more excited with each passing second. She didn't have enough time to look around her either. All she knew was that she was being shoved backward through the broken door and into a large room that was shrouded in dense shadows.

"What are you doing?" she asked breathlessly.

Brody's hands were already groping her body and his mouth was close enough to her neck that his breath tickled her skin when he said, "I'm taking you. Right here and now." And when he spoke, Brody pushed her up against a wall and reached to pull her skirts up around her waist.

Although she'd wanted to say something else, Nicki's words caught in her throat when she felt his hands get

131

even closer to her bare skin. Brody had quickly hiked up her outer skirts and was now rubbing between her legs through the filmy material of her slip.

The area between her legs was hot and wet, which only made Brody intensify his efforts to get through the last stubborn layer of clothing that stood between himself and the pleasure he was seeking. With one hand, he pulled open his pants and before he could free himself from his own garments, Brody felt Nicki's hands slipping beneath them, searching to get a hold on his stiff column of flesh.

Both of them started grunting and breathing heavier as they gave in to their basest of desires. Brody was first to give in fully to his animal instincts and took hold of her slip in both hands so he could rip it apart and then pull it from her body. Nicki let out an excited groan when she felt the clothes being torn off her body and forced Brody's pants down so she could wrap both hands around his cock.

Brody slipped both hands beneath her skirts and cupped Nicki's round backside so he could lift her up off her feet, pressing her even harder against the wall. The instant Nicki felt that, she pulled her feet up and wrapped her legs around his waist. Using one hand along with the motion of her hips, she fit him inside of her and then cinched her legs even tighter around him.

Brody felt a burning in his chest and soon realized that he'd been breathing in short, ragged bursts. When he felt Nicki's hands guide his penis between her legs and then felt the warm dampness of her body enveloping his, he let out that breath while pushing deeper into her. Nicki sighed deeply as well, her eyes widening as she felt his hard cock drive all the way up inside her body, touching her most sensitive spots before he couldn't go in any further.

Holding onto the back of his neck with one hand, Nicki somehow managed to loosen the ties on the top of her dress, which allowed her to pull it down to her stomach.

The instant her breasts were exposed, she felt Brody's lips on them, kissing her fiercely until he closed his teeth around her nipples.

Nicki pressed her shoulders against the wall so she could arch her back. She used her free hand to press his face deeper between her breasts and felt her entire body slamming repeatedly against the wall as he thrust forcefully between her open legs. Every stroke gave her a chill and every impact against the wall made a loud thumping sound, which, deep down inside, she hoped could be heard from the street.

Every one of Brody's senses were filled with her. All he could see was Nicki's bare, heaving breasts. All he could smell was the raw scent of her sex and all he could feel was his skin pressed against hers, sliding into hers, rubbing over hers. Every time he pushed his hips forward, Brody could feel Nicki's body giving in to him. And listening to her moans of passion only inspired him to thrust harder and faster until both of them were groaning out loud.

"Oh god," Nicki moaned. "Just like that. Keep it up. Right there."

At her direction, Brody kept up his pace and rhythm until he could feel the muscles in Nicki's vagina tightening around him. Now she pumped her hips in time with his, grinding her clitoris against the top of his shaft as he thrust into her again and again.

Finally, she clenched her eyes shut and pushed the back of her head against the wall as the first wave of her orgasm pulsed throughout her body. The force of it made her draw in a deep, gasping breath, which she held as every one of her muscles tingled with her climax.

It took every ounce of self-control Brody could muster to slow himself down as Nicki's nails raked over his shoulders. And at the last possible second, he eased almost completely out of her, only to thrust back in, which caused her eyes to snap open and her voice to echo through the empty store.

Nicki lowered her feet to the floor and pushed Brody back with the palms of her hands against his chest. She saw the warning glare in his eyes, reminding her of a feral wolf that was about to get the meat taken from its mouth. The fact that Brody wanted her so badly made Nicki's orgasm linger just a bit longer as she turned them both around so that it was Brody who had his back against the wall.

"Don't worry," she whispered. "I'm not through with you yet."

And with that, she took his penis in both hands, lowered herself to her knees in front of him and wrapped her lips around the tip of his cock.

Brody desperately wanted to feel her legs wrapped around him again while he thrust between her thighs. But the instant he felt her tongue gently glide along the bottom of his shaft, those longings were quickly forgotten.

She took him in her mouth with slow deliberation at first, closing her lips around the base of his stiff member and then running them all the way to its tip. Before long, she was bobbing her head back and forth, sucking on him loudly and swirling her tongue in circles over his sensitive flesh. When she felt his hands clasp around the back of her head, she took him all the way in her mouth and urged him to a climax with the expert motions of her tongue.

Minutes later, they emerged from the storefront. Both of them were smiling broadly and neither one paid the slightest attention to the looks they got from some of the locals who'd been standing across the street the entire time.

THIRTY-FOUR

The day passed quickly into dusk as the sun went down amid a thick range of colors from a dull orange to a few minutes of striking purple. Clint spent the last hours of daylight standing in various spots around the perimeter of the bank. Moving when he felt that he might start to get noticed, he always kept his eye on the men from Brody's crew, who he could pick out after a few hours of practice.

The gunmen were good at blending in with the crowd. Even when the amount of people started to thin out after business hours, they found spots from which they could watch the building without attracting too much attention. Sometimes, they would get up and walk away, only to reappear again after having circled the building a few times in between the patrols of armed guards who marched around the bank in shifts.

It was during this time that Clint realized these killers were truly in their element. While they'd seemed deadly enough while kidnapping Jeremiah Garver, they now seemed to move flawlessly while going about their tasks of collecting information and observing their opposition. If Clint hadn't known exactly what, or sometimes who, to look for, he might have been just as clueless as the

135

locals and the guards. Brody's men moved among them perfectly: hidden enough to keep their faces from being casually recognized and exposed enough to avoid looking suspicious.

At first, Clint had been nervous that the outlaws might hit the bank before he'd gotten a chance to watch them for a bit and form some kind of plan. But as the sun dropped below the western horizon, those fears faded along with the light. And when darkness fell over Haddleville, Clint felt somewhat relieved if not completely at ease.

He'd seen a few gangs move with such certainty and precision, but all of them had had some kind of ace up their sleeve. Whether that was a lawman in their pocket or some kind of inside information, Clint wasn't about to speculate. What he did know was that it would be a mistake to go to anyone else for help in case that person went straight to Brody.

Clint didn't like assuming that the local law was crooked, but with a man's life hanging in the balance and two children counting on him to bring their father home, he didn't want to take any chances whatsoever. Besides, the more Clint watched them, the more he thought he could spot a weakness in the way they functioned.

Like a military unit, the gunmen were a well-oiled machine that went about its business with exact precision. Every man had their job and knew it like second nature. And like every other machine, in order for it to run well, it had to have all of its parts intact. Therefore, the best plan that came to Clint's mind was also one of the simplest. In order to make sure the machine didn't work well, he had to sabotage enough of its parts, which would hopefully allow it to break down when it was under the most strain.

Clint pictured it in his mind like a train speeding down the tracks toward its destination. All he had to do was jam up the engine so that it fell apart when it was needed most. At that point, once he got the process of destruction in place, he could just sit back and watch the whole thing break apart in a ball of flame.

It wasn't the most elegant of plans, but it seemed to fit the situation rather nicely. Also, it was something that would be best suited for a man working on his own. That way, Clint could slip in whenever he wanted to do his damage and slip back out again when he was finished without having to worry about partners or anyone else getting in the way.

There were fewer loose ends and a smaller trail for the killers to follow once they knew they were being picked apart. Clint watched as another small group of the gunmen strode down Second Avenue toward the bank, a look of smug confidence etched onto their faces.

It would be a pleasure to wipe those smiles off their mouths and an even bigger pleasure to be there when they started falling apart enough to begin tearing at one another. Because he was dealing with a group of violent criminals who had naturally suspicious minds, Clint knew that they would start turning on one another eventually once things stopped going their way.

He watched as the fresher group walked next to the other and exchanged whatever signal they used to let the first group know it was time for them to take over. The process was subtle, but quickly executed as the new gunmen eased into position while the group being relieved dispersed into the crowd. To the untrained eye, it looked like nothing more than pedestrians shuffling about on the street.

But Clint knew exactly what he was seeing. More than that, he recognized it as the perfect opportunity to implement his own plan while the gunmen were comfortable in their anonymity. He watched them until the last possible second, tipping his hat over his eyes just as some of the gunmen moved past him on their way down Cottonwood.

Using the same techniques as the gunmen, Clint made himself part of the crowd and therefore nearly invisible to anyone who wasn't specifically looking for him. That fact struck Clint as ironic since it was those tried and proven tactics that would be used to bring about the robbers' eventual downfall. He waited until Brody's men walked past him before turning around and falling into step behind them.

Although he was no bank robber, Clint knew that he had some time before Brody made his play. First of all, if they were getting closer to the time of the actual robbery, Clint would have caught sight of Brody himself by now. Second, the robbers seemed too relaxed to be minutes away from their big strike. And third, this was not the best time to pull the job.

Clint had been watching the bank long enough himself to know that the guards wouldn't be changing shifts for another few hours at least. And that, combined with the fact that there were still a lot of workers and customers filing out of the building before the doors closed, told Clint that any robber would hold off for a while until they could take up their positions without tipping their hand.

It was getting more than a little strange for Clint to be thinking so much like a criminal. As he followed the small group of gunmen up the street he felt somehow connected to them. It was almost as though he was as much a part of this job as they were—the only difference being that his part was to make sure it failed.

Tailing the robbers, Clint raced through a mental list of everything else he needed to do. Although he knew he had a little time before the robbery, he wasn't sure exactly how long he did have. He hoped that Brody would want to give his men some rest before hitting the bank. Despite the fact that he didn't want to make too many dangerous assumptions, he had to make the occasional leap of faith simply because he was one man taking on a small army.

There was also the children to think about. In all the time he'd fallen into the role of watchdog to the gang, Clint hadn't allowed himself to forget that Kyle and Sadie were waiting in the boardinghouse for him to return. He'd already had enough experience with them to know they had a hard time keeping in one place for too long. He silently cursed at himself for not checking in with them sooner, but now it was too late.

The gunmen appeared to be collecting the rest of their group and were heading toward Haddleville's saloon district, and Clint couldn't have asked for a better time to confront them. Tired after several hours of circling their target and still fresh from the morning's ride, the killers were prime targets.

As much as Clint hated to leave the children alone much longer, he knew he had to trust them a little bit if he was going to make it out of Haddleville alive. One slip or mental lapse in this game, and a player would lose their life.

THIRTY-FIVE

Clint followed the group of gunmen, which eventually grew to four members. The killers gathered all together in front of a saloon less than three blocks away from the bank. As he made his way closer to them, Clint could hear the gunmen discussing what they'd seen and how easy the bank robbery was going to move.

Although the gang members might have been a little full of themselves, Clint figured they had every right to be. Judging by the way they were talking and what he'd seen with his own eyes, the security around the bank had become only a shadow of what it had once been. The institution seemed to be relying more on its reputation for being impenetrable than the practices that had once made it so.

Shaking his head, Clint hoped that whoever was in charge of bank security would take a lesson from what was about to happen. He would have considered tipping them off himself if he knew someone inside the bank he was absolutely certain he could trust. Making sure to keep a good distance between himself and the gunmen, Clint kept an eye on them as they entered the saloon, walked up to the bar, and ordered another round of drinks.

Go ahead and let them drink, Clint thought. That would just make his job that much easier.

Not even half an hour went by before the four gang members grew tired of the saloon and drifted back out into the street. It spooked Clint when he figured they would want to keep the excitement flowing through their veins by getting a taste of Haddleville's gambling halls. The eerie part wasn't in making the prediction, but in the fact that he was quickly proven right.

The four men left the saloon and went straight for the closest poker parlor they could find, which was a place called The Double Deuce built right across the street from the saloon. Clint didn't doubt that the gambling hall got most of their business from customers who mistook the warm buzz of alcohol for the caress of Lady Luck upon their brow. Seeing that The Double Deuce was darker, slightly more crowded, and noisier than the saloon, Clint was more than happy to let the gunmen walk into the place and get themselves nice and comfortable.

Once he saw the others were situated, Clint stepped inside as well. He watched the gunmen out of the corner of his eye while walking up to a group of women standing near the front door, advertising their wares through the use of low-cut dresses and bright red lipstick.

Clint stepped up to the women and knew he was on the right track when all three of them latched onto him like mosquitoes on an exposed jugular. "How would you ladies like to make some easy money?" he asked.

A short blonde with slender legs and an impressive bustline was first to answer. "Always, handsome," she said while moving up to Clint and running her hands over his chest. "Did you want us all together or one at a time?"

"We don't mind sharing you in the same bed," a brunette with longer legs and a trimmer frame chimed in. "But it'll cost you extra."

As if on cue, the third woman walked up to him and

wrapped her arms around the other two. This one had lighter blond hair and displayed the most generous curves of them all. She let her hair fall over her shoulders and licked her upper lip invitingly before saying, "It's extra, but make no mistake . . . we're worth every last penny."

Although Clint had much more important things to worry about and wasn't the type to pay for a woman's favor anyway, he was still a man and couldn't help but let his mind wander with the possibilities he was hearing. The women no doubt sensed this and writhed against one another in a provocative display.

Clint shook the enticing images from his mind in a supreme show of self-control. "That's not exactly what I had in mind," he said, even though the rest of his body was screaming for him to set everything else aside.

"Oh really?" the second blonde asked. "Well, if it's anything dirtier you want, there's a Chinese cathouse on Fifth that caters to a more discerning crowd."

Shaking his head, Clint realized that his conversation was starting to draw attention from the people around him and that set his mind back on its original course. "That's not it, either. All I need is a few moments of your time and a bit of your persuasive powers and you will have more than earned this." With that, Clint produced a folded ten-dollar bill from his pocket and held it in front of him.

The ladies glanced at one another and nodded before the brunette reached out to pluck the bill deftly from between Clint's fingers. "All right," she said. "You've got our attention."

THIRTY-SIX

"Can you cover a marker that big?" the house dealer at the head of the table asked. He was looking at one of the four men who'd taken up seats at a game of five-card stud.

Until now, the game had been low stakes and easygoing with only two other players adding to the pot. But in the space of one hand, the new arrivals had insisted on upping the ante far enough to make the dealer hold back before doling out the next round of cards.

"Of course I can handle it," Ford Fargo said with a sneer that failed to impress the dealer. "What's the matter? Too rich for this dump?"

The dealer seemed used to this kind of talk and merely rolled his eyes when he heard it coming from Ford. "It's house policy, sir," the dealer said without trying to hide his exasperation. "I'll just need to see some of your cash before I can cover the bet you just made."

Scowling angrily, Ford stood up and glared across the table at the dealer. "There ain't nobody who can talk to me like that," he said, even though the other three men who'd come in with him seemed almost ready to differ. "And I surely won't take it from the likes of you."

All four gunmen were on their feet before the dealer

started looking genuinely uncomfortable. Each of them had their hands near their guns, but neither had drawn just yet. Ford was about to spout off some more when he caught the flicker of movement in the corner of his eye.

Assuming that his friends would handle whoever was coming, Ford said, "Just deal the cards and shut up."

But the dealer seemed preoccupied all of a sudden. His eyes drifted toward something to Ford's right.

"I said—"

"Hey, Ford," one of the other gunmen interrupted. "Why don't you put a cork in it and pay attention?"

Ford was just about to get himself riled up even further when he wheeled around to chew out his partner. The moment he turned, however, the insult he'd prepared stuck in his throat. What he saw was more than enough to take the rest of his breath away to boot.

"Hello, boys," the brunette said while locking her eyes on Ford and advancing toward him as though he was the catch of the day.

Standing on either side of the brunette, both of the blondes reached out and placed their hands upon the gunmen in just the right way to make them almost forget what they were doing in Haddleville before meeting them. The shorter blonde divided her attention between two of the killers while the tall blonde and the brunette each took one for themselves.

"Well, what have we here?" Ford asked, his face brightening with a wide smile.

The brunette leaned in to chew on his earlobe while one hand drifted down to his crotch. "If you don't know, then I think I've got a real nice surprise for you."

Ford couldn't get away from the table fast enough. All three of the remaining gunmen were right behind him as the ladies led them off to a set of doors at the back of the room. The gunmen didn't get more than the women's names before they were standing in front of those doors being showered with breathtaking kisses.

"The party's in there," the brunette said with a mischievous gleam in her eyes.

"Is there another one of your friends in there?" one of the gunmen asked. "Or do one of you have to take two of us on?"

The short blonde winked and slapped two of the men on their rear. "I think one of us could take all of you on," she said without showing the slightest bit of doubt. "But there's something even better waiting for you in there."

"Really?" Ford said. "How much is it gonna cost us?"

The brunette wriggled against him and pinched his cheek. "For a bunch of men like you . . . it won't cost a thing. That part's already been taken care of. It's a little gift from your boss."

That brought delighted smiles to all of the gunmen's faces. Ford was already pulling open the door when he said, "Hot damn, that Brody sure knows how to treat his crew."

All of the gunmen were through the door and standing in a dark room before they realized the ladies hadn't followed them in. When they tried to look over their shoulders to check on them, all they got for their trouble was a door slammed shut in their faces.

"What the hell?"

Suddenly, a lantern flared up at the back of the room. For a moment, all of the gunmen were blinded by the light which had appeared from nowhere in the total blackness. They all raised their arms to instinctively protect their eyes from the glare and when they lowered them again, they saw a solitary figure standing in front of them.

"Hello, boys," Clint said.

THIRTY-SEVEN

Of the four gunmen, only two of them had actually gotten
a look at Clint up close back when they'd crossed paths
at Jeremiah's house. Ford and one of the others had been
guarding the place when they'd been rudely introduced to
the butt of Clint's gun. Because of this, they were the
only ones to recognize what had happened the moment
they got a look at the man who'd appeared from the darkness.

The other two knew Clint by the results of his work
only and were still wondering how come the three ladies
hadn't chosen to join them inside the room.

"Holy shit," Ford grunted as he fumbled for his gun.
"It's him."

That was enough to spark the rest into action and in
the space of a second or two, everyone inside the cramped
quarters was moving in a different direction. The room
was bigger than a closet, but smaller than an average hotel
room. Used mostly for storage, it was lined with shelves
along both walls and the entire perimeter was stacked with
dusty crates and stacks of various signs or papers. It had
been crowded enough just by having five grown men inside it when they were standing still. Now that they were

all moving, the space was quickly running out.

Clint was counting on the fact that they would all charge for him at once. And after they'd all gotten a good look at him, the gunmen didn't disappoint. Waiting until the last moment, Clint lowered his head and held out his arms as if he was going to embrace one of them. Instead, he rushed straight for them and threw his shoulder into it at the last second, catching two of the men in their sides.

Both of those two gunmen got all the air knocked from their lungs upon impact. While both of them had managed to get a hold of their pistols and get their fingers through the trigger guards, neither of them were able to clear leather. The man that got hit by Clint's left shoulder was spun on the balls of his feet and shoved to the side, while the one to Clint's right was knocked completely off his feet, bouncing his spine against a row of hard wooden shelves.

Having seen Clint in action once before, Ford and his partner knew enough to step back as soon as they saw him start to charge. Rather than make the mistake of getting close to him, they pulled their guns and took aim. They would have squeezed off a shot or two if not for the fact that Clint was still in a tangle with their other two partners.

Ford sighted down the barrel of his pistol and thumbed back the hammer.

Hearing the metallic click and seeing the glint of light upon steel, Clint acted reflexively and all but tossed himself at the gunman who was about to fire. He reached out with both hands while throwing himself into the line of fire, the possibility of failure not even entering his mind. If Clint had hesitated for less than a second, he wouldn't have done anything but present Ford with a bigger target.

As it was, Clint felt the touch of steel against his fingertips, strained to reach out a little farther, and finally clamped his fist around the middle section of Ford's gun.

In one fluid motion, he ducked down with his knees and pushed up with his arm, twisting his wrist until the pistol was turned around to aim at the man who'd been holding it.

The shot was forced and at an awkward angle, but it had its desired effect. When Ford's gun went off, it filled the room with a deafening explosion along with a cloud of black smoke. Ford had tried to keep hold of his weapon, but made the mistake of holding on too tight and got his wrist fractured for his troubles. When the bullet sped from the chamber, it dug a bloody trench into the side of his face and took off most of his right ear before burying itself into the wall.

Clint wheeled around on the balls of his feet to get a look at what the other gunmen were doing behind his back. Both of the men he'd bull-rushed were just getting to their feet and the third was staring back at him over the length of his gun barrel.

At that moment, Clint's mind set aside everything else in that room except for that one man in front of him and the gun that was about to go off in his hand. Clint moved solely on reflex, thumbing back the trigger to the gun he'd taken, pointing it toward the other man and squeezing the trigger.

Both guns appeared to go off at the same time. But Clint had taken his shot a split second faster, which was all he needed to send a bullet into the gunman's chest just as he was taking his shot. The round's impact was enough to crumple the gang member over as the chunk of lead punched through his rib cage and burrowed all the way through to his heart. By the time his finger clenched around his trigger, his aim had been pulled to one side, sending his bullet through a piece of Clint's shirt without touching his flesh.

Clint knew better than to take any time to relish his victory or even thank whatever lucky stars had been hanging over him. Instead, he turned his body in a tight spiral that sent him twisting to his left while dropping him down to one knee. The maneuver was completed just as another pair of shots blasted through the cramped room; one whipping through the air over Clint's head and another ripping a nasty gash at the spot where his left shoulder met his neck.

Using his momentum, Clint kept his body turning in the same direction and snapped his right arm out like a whip. Once it was fully extended, he let go of Ford's gun and sent the pistol flying into the face of the gunman he'd knocked down in his initial charge.

The gun slammed into its target's face with a bone-crunching impact. Even before it had a chance to drop to the floor, the gun was awash in fresh blood that flowed from the man's busted nose. The man standing next to the first gunman stepped to one side as his partner once again toppled to the floor.

Clint's hand hovered over the handle of his Colt like a deadly promise only seconds away from being fulfilled. "I'm giving the rest of you a chance," he said. "Give up right now or you'll wind up like your friend over there with the hole in his chest."

Glancing between each other, none of the gunmen seemed tempted by the offer in the least. Even though the man with the broken nose was already making a desperate grab for his weapon, the pain coursing through his skull was enough to throw every part of him out of kilter and his hands merely knocked the pistol from its holster to where it clattered toward a stack of nearby boxes.

Clint kept his eyes trained on the two men in front of him, watching Ford out of the corner of his eye. As he'd planned, Clint saw Ford taking advantage of his position by trying to attack him from behind. All Clint had to see was the movement of Ford's arm and the sight of a gun before he drew the Colt, pointed it at Ford, and drilled a hole through the gunman's face . . . all without taking his eyes from the remaining two gunmen.

Keeping his gun aimed toward the front of the room, Clint faced the other direction and said, "Two down. Care to test me with the new odds?"

"And why the hell shouldn't we?" the gunman whose face was still intact asked. "You're just gonna kill us anyway."

Moving his arm back slowly, Clint turned the Colt's barrel toward the floor and holstered it. "Oh, but that's where you're mistaken. Do you think I'd waste those girls' talents just to toss you fellas in here? I can think of plenty of other things for them to do, but my business with you is much more important." Suddenly, Clint thought back to the way the brunette had know exactly where to touch him when she came in close. "Well, more important for the moment, anyway."

THIRTY-EIGHT

The gunman with the broken nose finally managed to stand up once he'd abandoned the effort of trying to retrieve his weapon. Even though he was back on his feet, he was everything but steady and wobbled as though he had a gut full of whiskey. "Tho mhat's the deal?" he asked through a mask of blood.

"Take a vacation," Clint said plainly. "I don't care where you go, just make sure it's very far away from here and that it starts right now."

Both of the robbers looked at each other and quickly made their decision.

The one on Clint's left was the one to move first since his actions weren't impeded by any injury more severe than a few bruised ribs. He slapped his hand against the handle of his gun and had it halfway from the holster before Clint stepped forward and grabbed him by the wrist. Wrenching the gunman's hand in the wrong direction, Clint forced him to let go of the pistol and then punched him in the stomach with his left hand. That doubled the gunman over just in time for Clint to raise his left knee and pound it into the gunman's face.

Seeing that he'd dropped one of the killers, Clint turned

151

to face the one whose nose he'd broken. Apparently, that gunman wasn't about to be caught a third time and had taken a few steps back until his shoulders bumped against the shelves in the rear of the room. Once he'd put some space between himself and Clint, the gunman reached around behind him and pulled a Bowie knife from a scabbard hidden at the base of his spine. He seemed to be using his pain as an incentive rather than allowing it to stand in his way any longer and his steps were getting steadier by the second.

By the time Clint saw the foot-long blade, it was too late for him to stop the killer from flipping it once in his hand and throwing it at him. Clint did manage to move back a step or two and by the time the knife left the killer's hand, Clint had drawn the Colt and pulled the trigger.

There was a blast of gunfire, followed by a sharp ping of lead on metal, followed by a small burst of sparks where bullet and blade met no more than a few feet from Clint's body. Instinctively closing his eyes and turning his head, Clint wasn't quite fast enough to avoid a few bits of stray metal that had chipped off the blade. The slivers bit into his face and neck like bee stings, but he ignored the pain and got ready to face the killer's next attack.

"Vuck you," the gunman with the broken nose spat with a painful slur. He'd managed to pick up the weapon his partner had dropped and was less than a second away from pulling the trigger.

Clint had enough time to wonder why he'd even gone through all the trouble of trying to keep these men alive in the first place when it would have been so much easier to gun them down like ducks in a row. This man, even more than the others, should have known that he was damn lucky to be alive. But what did he decide to do after all the chances he'd been given?

Throw them away.

Fight rather than flee.

Shoot before bargaining or even waiting for a chance to escape.

The reason he'd given them the chances, Clint thought as he aimed the Colt and fired, was because he wasn't like those killers. Despite the fact that he killed, he only did so whenever it was necessary. And every time was just as hard as the first.

Clint's shot rang out alone. The man with the broken nose didn't even get his finger clenched all the way before a piece of lead dug a tunnel through his chest and dropped him into a pile on the floor.

Clint shook his head and reloaded his Colt. The last gunman still breathing was just starting to come around again. Before he opened his eyes, he felt a slight breeze pass by his hand as Clint kicked the gun out of his reach.

"Come on," Clint said as he reached down and grabbed a handful of the gunman's shirt. Lifting him to his feet as though he was handling a cat by the scruff of its neck, Clint tossed the killer toward one side of the room.

The gunman backpedaled a few feet before the backs of his knees bumped against a row of boxes. He started to fall backward, but landed roughly on his backside on top of the wooden crates. Having just shaken off his temporary unconsciousness, the gunman felt as though the world was spinning around him and tilting madly upon its axis. Even when he came to a rest with his back against the wall, he had to press his hands to his forehead to try and stop the confusion.

"What's going on?" the gunman said groggily.

Clint snapped the Colt's cylinder shut and dropped it into the holster at his side. "Shut up and listen to me," he said.

Glancing around the room, the gunman's eyes went wide as he spotted the bodies of all three of his companions. "I . . . I'll leave here right now. I'll leave town and never come back and tell Brody to go to—"

"The time for that's over." Although Clint knew the fight hadn't taken more than a minute or two, he was certain the gunshots would be more than enough to attract unwanted attention. "If you didn't take that deal when I first offered it, you won't take it now. That means you'll just go running back to Brody if I let you go." Intensifying his stare, Clint asked, "So what should I do with you, then?"

Letting the gunman's fear sink in a bit more, Clint stepped back and crossed his arms over his chest. "Maybe I should march you straight into the sheriff's office. My guess is that the law's got their eyes open for Brody and any of his men in this whole part of the country."

The gunman started to say something, but held back. He paused for a moment, the adrenaline and tension coursing through his body like wildfire, and shifted his eyes back to Clint.

And it was in that very moment that Clint got what he'd been after. Staring into the gunman's eyes, studying them with all the subtle skill of a true gambler sizing up his opponent, Clint watched the killer's response to that threat and saw something that answered a question that had been bugging him for a while.

The killer looked scared of Clint, that much was certain. He was also angry as hell that his friends had been shot. But when Clint mentioned the sheriff, the killer didn't display the slightest bit of fear or even reluctance to be in a cage.

It was as though a part of him was hoping he'd see the sheriff. But more than that, the gunman looked as though he'd just been dealt the one card he needed to fill an inside straight flush.

That confirmed something that Clint had suspected ever since he'd figured out what Brody was doing in Haddle-ville: the town's law had to be crooked.

It wasn't too hard to figure that the gunman might prefer to go to jail rather than meet his maker, but that wouldn't explain the definite look of victory Clint had seen written all over his face, if only for less than a second. Clint had seen plenty of men look relieved to be turned over to the law if that meant living to see another day. They would also look at least mildly perturbed at the prospect of losing their freedom. But this man was neither. Instead, he looked as though he was being handed over to a friend.

And that split second of loaded silence was all Clint needed to feel he'd accomplished something.

"Thanks a lot," Clint said to the gunman.

"So that's it? I'll be headed to the sheriff's now?"

"Nope. I changed my mind."

Hearing that, the killer's face dropped and every bit of hope he might have had melted away like last year's snowfall.

THIRTY-NINE

The Double Deuce was never the quietest spot in Haddleville, but normally the noise inside the place could be contained within its walls. On this particular night, however, raucous shouting and brusque laughter rattled the walls, shook the windows in their panes, and sent tremors through the rows of glasses hanging over the bar.

Once Clint was finished with what he was doing inside the storage room, he couldn't help but notice the sounds. At first, he thought that a posse was stampeding through the place on its way to drag him outside, or that perhaps Brody was bringing the rest of his gang to come to aid his men.

But posses didn't usually laugh so hard when they were out on duty. And outlaw gangs normally didn't sing when they were about to charge into a fight.

"Is someone singing?" Clint asked himself in confusion.

For a moment, Clint thought that the air was getting thin inside the enclosed space and he was hearing things. It wasn't uncommon for miners to have their minds play tricks on them if they didn't come up for air enough. But when Clint took a deep breath, he knew his mind was perfectly fine, which meant that he was indeed hearing singing echo through the very boards that made up the building.

It wouldn't have been out of place in a showroom or maybe even a saloon. But gamblers tended to like their places a bit more quiet. It made it easier to concentrate that way. Now that he could move around without having to worry about the gunmen, Clint walked up to the door, opened it and took a peek outside.

The first thing he saw was a pair of rounded backsides covered in ruffles and lace being shaken fast enough that his eyes had trouble following them. Looking up, he saw two familiar blond heads of hair, and in front of them, there was the brunette.

All three ladies danced on top of a pair of card tables, kicking their heels up and swinging their hair around in a display that was almost wild enough to explain why everyone was so worked up. But dancing girls were nothing new in most places, even ones as exceptional as these. Clint was just starting to wonder what all the commotion was about when all three girls spun around on the balls of their feet to face him, twirling their skirts up almost to their waists.

Clint felt his jaw drop open when he caught sight of the trio's smooth, silky legs, strong thighs, as well as the soft thatch of pubic hair between them. The shorter blonde spotted Clint and winked at him moments before all three took hold of their skirts, bent at the waist and gave the entire room a lingering glance at their perfectly rounded bottoms.

The taller blonde and the brunette straightened up and spun back around to face the crowd once again, but the shorter blonde stayed bent over. Her face was only inches away from Clint's so she leaned in a bit more to plant a kiss upon his forehead.

"Thought you could use a distraction," she said with a wink. "The least we could do was oblige."

Before Clint could utter a word of thanks, the blonde stood up and joined the other two. In perfect coordination, they let out a full-throated cheer that was immediately returned by the crowd and then kicked their legs high into the air. When their feet reached the highest point, every man in the crowd let out another one of those cries that had been threatening to bring the place down around their ears.

Clint waited until the girls turned around again and caught the blonde's attention. "Where's the back door?" he asked when she bent down to his level.

The short blonde nodded toward one of the far corners.

"Thanks a lot," Clint said once he spotted the exit. "Just let me get something out of here and you can stop."

Grinning mischievously, the blonde said, "Stop, hell! We're making more money tonight than we have in a long time!"

This time when they spun around a got ready to kick, the girls showed Clint something else besides the fact that they weren't wearing any underwear. Each of their garters were stuffed with folded bills that ruffled up around the tops of their thighs like freshly minted feathers. Before Clint could step back into the storage room, he saw one of the gamblers walk up to the brunette and add another bill to her collection.

Clint was laughing to himself as he went back into the other room and walked over to the gunman he'd hogtied and left in the corner.

Somehow, the killer had managed to work the bandanna that Clint had stuffed into his mouth down to his chin using his tongue and jaw muscles. "Brody'll know I'm gone, you son of a bitch," the killer said, now that he'd had a chance to work himself up into a lather. "You can't just shoot down three men and walk out without anyone on the other side of that door hearing you!"

Taking hold of the gunman by the ropes connecting his feet and hands, Clint dragged him toward the door. "You know something? On any other night I'd have to agree with you. But this time . . . I think I just might have a chance to escape your boss's all-seeing eyes."

As soon as he opened the door, Clint and his prisoner both got a breathtaking view as the ladies on top of the tables spun around and kicked their skirts up in the air. Suddenly, the killer forgot the threat he was going to toss at his captor. And even though Clint had seen them before, he still had to stop for a moment and watch the exotic twirls again.

"All right," Clint said once he was able to snap himself out of the women's trance. "Time to go."

And with that, Clint hefted the gunman to his feet and dragged him out The Double Deuce's back door. He drew a few curious glances, but only just as he was leaving the building. And the few who'd spotted him were quickly distracted by some personal attention from the dancers.

FORTY

Clint returned to the gambling hall half an hour later. Although the rowdy dance number was over and The Double Deuce was back to its normal atmosphere, the three ladies weren't hard to find since they were surrounded by admirers. But as soon as Clint walked past them, the brunette excused herself and followed him to an empty space at the bar.

"Not to be ungrateful," he said once he'd shooed away the barkeep. "But I feel like I got a whole lot more than I paid for."

The dancer waved off the comment and smiled. Shifting her skirts to one side so that the slit running up almost to her thigh opened to reveal her stuffed garter, she ran her fingers over the folded bills and said, "Don't fret yourself. Actually, I think we might be doing that more often."

"Well, my name's Clint, and you have my thanks."

The dancer let her dress fall back into place and took the hand he offered. "I'm Dulcy. And as far as us covering your behind back there, don't get a swelled head and think that we did it just to protect that pretty hide of yours. Brody's been bringing his scum in here for some time. All of us working girls recognize them the minute they walk in and believe me when I tell you that it's not for any good reasons."

"They get a little rough?" Clint asked.

"No. Actually they get a lot rough. It didn't take much to know that someone wanting to lure them into a trap in an empty room didn't have any kind intentions in mind. And whoever wanted to bring a bit of harm to those boys is all right by us.

"Celina was listening in on the other side of the door," Dulcy confessed, pointing to the short blonde. "And when we knew there was going to be shooting, we whipped up a little something to drown out all that noise."

"There . . . ahhh . . . might be a bit of a mess in there."

Unaffected by the knowledge that the mess he referred to was actually three dead bodies, Dulcy shrugged and replied, "Nobody should go in that room for at least a few more hours. Besides, it won't be the first time the owners found surprises like that. They'll just assume they were another couple of cheaters who got what's coming to them. Since they know Brody's gang as well as we do, they probably won't be too shocked.

"And don't worry about the law neither. The sheriff's awful understanding about matters like that," Dulcy added with a conspiratorial tone in her voice.

Clint nodded appreciatively and smiled, his theory about the law in Haddleville confirmed. "Well, at least let me buy you a drink."

"Much as I'd like to accept, our dance card is full right now. But if you have some other time in mind . . . I'd be happy to make sure I'm available. No charge of course."

"As tempting as that is, I'll have to say no. You're not the only one with a whole lot of work ahead of them."

Dulcy nodded and was about to leave when she stopped and leaned in close so she could whisper in Clint's ear. "If you don't mind me askin', what did you do with that fella you carted out of here?"

"He's cooling his heels in a room I paid for through the next two days. The hotel I picked didn't seem like the town's best and I made sure they knew their guests wouldn't want to be disturbed."

"You got more of them?"

"Not yet," Clint said. "But soon. Real soon."

Smiling and running her eyes over Clint from head to toe, Dulcy gave him a kiss on the cheek. "I like your style, Clint."

"And I like your . . . performance. Next time I'm in town, I'll be sure to stop by to take in the next one."

"You do that. And if you let me know ahead of time, I'll give you a private show that you won't soon forget."

Dulcy reached down to smack Clint on the backside and then spun around to join the two blondes. It took her less than a second to work her way back in with the group of men and become the only thing on their minds.

Clint received a wave or a wink in passing from all the of the girls as he walked to the front door and stepped outside. The sun was long gone and the night had the flavor of already being more than halfway over when the truth was far from that. The night was still in its youth and Clint was a long way from the next time he could rest.

FORTY-ONE

Despite the fact that he had much to do and probably little time in which to do it, Clint walked down the street and made his way to Mrs. Brasser's boardinghouse. He only had to get in sight of the front porch before he was reminded about why he was going through all this trouble in the first place.

Sitting there, with his chin resting on his hands, Kyle waited patiently, sleep weighing heavily on his eyes.

"Shouldn't you be in bed?" Clint asked as he climbed the steps and took a seat next to the boy.

Kyle shrugged his shoulders. "Yes. I snuck out."

"Couldn't sleep?"

"No, sir," the boy replied, even though his weary eyes and slumped posture told a different story. "I knew you didn't come back yet and I wanted to be here when you did."

"That's good to hear. It's always nice to be missed."

"I know you're going after the men that took my pa and I want to go with you."

Clint started to protest, but he was cut off before he could even get a word out. Suddenly brimming with energy, Kyle sat up straight and his eyes glistened anxiously.

"I can hide from them, Clint. They'll never see me. You know that's true. And . . . and I can shoot a gun. Pa always told me I was a good shot. With both of us, we can find—"

Now it was Clint's turn to interrupt and he did so by grabbing hold of Kyle's shoulder. It might have been a little rough, but it stopped the boy in his tracks, which was what Clint felt he had to do. "Look here," Clint said sternly. "I know you and your sister have been through some hard times and I know you miss your father, but I don't ever want to hear you talk about using a gun against another person again. Do you understand me?"

Kyle nodded slowly at first and then lowered his chin back down onto his hands. "Yessir."

"Good." Softening his tone, Clint let go of Kyle's arm and put his around the boy's shoulders. "I'll help you and your pa, but no good comes out of hurting people."

"But sometimes, you have to prot—"

"And when you have to protect yourself, you do so. But if nobody picked up a gun in the first place, nobody would ever get hurt that way." Clint paused for a second and knew that he was getting through to the kid. "Look, since your father isn't here right now, I'll have to talk to you since you're the man of the family in his place."

Kyle definitely liked the sound of that and he perked right up.

"Everything has its price," Clint said. "I'll do this job for you and bring your father back, but not for nothing. You have to promise me to grow up to be a good man . . . not some gunfighter like those rats that took your father."

"But—"

"No buts. Promise me or I take you both home right now. Because if your father's any kind of man, he'd want you to grow up the same way. You know I'm right."

After a while, Kyle nodded. "Yeah. He told me that before."

"Good. Then promise me and I can get back to work."

"I promise."

"And you can get back to bed."

At that moment, the front door opened and Mrs. Brasser stepped out. She was clutching a shawl over her shoulders and all but pounced on Kyle the instant she saw him.

"Thank the lord above, there you are!" she said while scooping him effortlessly up off the porch. "I thought you'd run off or . . ." Glancing at Clint, she thought twice about finishing her sentence. ". . . or that you were out to sneak another piece of that blueberry pie you children liked so much."

Kyle looked back at Clint and as strange as it was to see a thirteen-year-old boy halfway dangling from the arms of an elderly woman who picked him up as though he were an infant, Clint looked back at him without cracking a smile. At least . . . he managed that much for about two seconds.

"I see you're in good hands," Clint said, while barely suppressing a laugh at Kyle's predicament. "I'll leave you both and check in tomorrow morning."

"You won't be getting some rest, Mr. Adams?" Mrs. Brasser asked.

"Not just yet, ma'am. But I'll be back for some of that pie as soon as I'm able. Thanks again for watching after the children for me. I can see they're . . . a handful."

"Not at all," the elderly woman replied, either missing or ignoring his pun. Setting Kyle down, she held open the front door for him. "I'll see to it that they're well fed and don't wander off," she said, swatting Kyle on the backside for emphasis.

Clint waited until the boy was inside the house before he stepped up to Mrs. Brasser and said in a lowered voice,

"There . . . uh . . . might be some people looking for the kids."

"You told me that much before."

"Yes, well, it looks like those people might be about to start some trouble and I just want to know if there's anything I can do now to help you. Or if there might be something extra I can—"

She cut him off with a raised hand. "I'll not accept a penny more from you, sir. Those children are angels and I'll do what I can to keep them out of harm's way. Tell you the truth, I saw the boy sitting out here and was about to bring him in . . . but he's been troubled all day. I thought he could use the fresh air."

"You're a godsend, ma'am. And do me a favor. Be sure to keep yourself inside until this all passes over. I'll be back when it's through."

"Excuse me for prying, but . . . until *what* passes over?"

"Believe me," Clint said while turning and walking away. "You'll know it when it happens."

FORTY-TWO

Jeremiah thought for certain he was going to be sick.

It wasn't brought on by anything he'd eaten or any of the terror he'd been forced to endure in the last couple of days. Instead, the cause of his ills was the smile he forced himself to wear and the friendly words he'd forced himself to say to the very men who'd torn his life apart.

Walking beside Brody's men and not tearing them apart with his bare hands took every ounce of strength Jeremiah could muster. And though he was a patient man with strength to spare, the effort of it all sat in his guts like a piece of rancid meat that his body refused to digest. And though he was a man who believed in fighting to protect his own and defend himself, Jeremiah knew the only real way he could do both of those things was to pretend he was going along with Brody's plan.

Just to make it all seem real, he'd asked all the questions he would have asked in the days when he'd actually been like Brody. In the days before meeting his dear departed Jenny, he would have been concerned with things like profit and risk factors. Details of the planned robbery would have consumed him and the only other thing on his mind would have been making sure the rest of the gang was prepared to hold up their end.

So, wearing the smile like a mask that was attached to his face by steel hooks, Jeremiah asked all the right questions and said all the right things to make Brody and his men believe that he was going along with the plan. They would never truly take him in as one of their own, but they might be put at ease enough to let their guard down . . . or at least give him some morsels of information that could be put to use at a later time.

Jeremiah was being watched by a group of four of Brody's killers. Together, they'd roamed the town and scouted out a few key locations. But they'd spent the lion's share of their evening watching the bank itself. Hiding like rats in a cellar, the gunmen had scurried in the shadows, observing the bank's guards as they walked around the building in their prearranged circles, not knowing the hell that was about to be unleashed upon them.

All the while, Jeremiah knew he was being watched as well. The gang members might not have been educated properly, but they were not stupid either. They took Jeremiah with them, putting him in positions where he might move against them or even make noise to draw the guards' attention. But Jeremiah knew better than to act unless he absolutely had to. Those same gunmen that had the noose around his neck were just waiting for an excuse to tighten it. One step in the wrong direction and Jeremiah was sure he'd feel a knife in his back or a bullet burning through his skull.

Jeremiah half expected to feel either of those at any time. Walking the fine line between life and death, teetering on it at every second, he felt his stomach churning inside of him and could taste the nervous bile in the back of his throat. In the old days, he would have never been so anxious, even about the possibility of dying. But now, he had something to look forward to. Someone to live for.

And a promise to keep.

Not only to Kyle and Sadie, but to Jenny as well. He swore to her that he would keep their children safe. In fact, that was one of the last things he'd gotten to say to his wife before she passed on. Remembering that, Jeremiah thought of something much worse than death: the very idea that, wherever she was, Jenny might look down on him with shame.

So he quelled the impulse to break free from the gunmen at his first opportunity. He would continue playing their games until he knew for certain that he could get away clean, get to his children, and take all of them away where no one could find them.

"What time is it?" one of the killers asked.

Jeremiah fished a small copper watch from his pocket and flipped open the lid. "Almost ten."

"Then get yer ass in gear and start movin' back to the hotel. We got about two hours before you start earnin' yer keep."

"The robbery's at midnight?" Jeremiah asked.

"Yeah. What's the matter . . . you don't remember what Brody told ya?"

On the contrary, Jeremiah had made it a point to remember every last thing that Brody had said, along with every useless word that came out of his gang members' mouths. Useless, that is, until this very moment.

"Oh, that's right," Jeremiah quickly replied. "Midnight."

The killer looked as though he thought Jeremiah was too stupid to live. He let out a snorting breath before motioning for the rest of their group to come over to where he and Jeremiah were standing. Having just come back from watching the bank, the killers were making their way toward the saloon district for some much needed muscle relaxers. "Come on. It's time we started heading back."

Grumbling under their breaths to one another, the re-

maining men had just been about to open the door to The
Double Deuce. "But there was supposed to be some kinda
show goin' on in there," one of them said.

"Forget that bullshit. You'll have plenty of time for
gettin' piss drunk when we're done doing what we came
here for."

Although none of them seemed happy about it, the
three moved away from the gambling hall's front door
and formed a tight circle around Jeremiah. As always,
they looked at their prisoner with disdain, but not nearly
as much as when they'd first met him.

"We'll be able to buy that place when we get done
cracking that vault," Jeremiah said, wearing the grin of a
coyote about to jump into a henhouse.

For a moment, the killers simply looked at Jeremiah as
though they were entertaining the thought of spitting in
his face. Then, after glancing around at their partners, they
all broke into raucous laughter while reaching out to slap
Jeremiah on the back.

"Hell," one of them said. "After tonight, we'll be able
to buy this whole damn town!"

They laughed together for a few seconds and then
started walking toward the Mason Dixon Hotel. And just
as suddenly as it started, the laughter came to a stop.
Every one of the killers stopped abruptly to glare into
Jeremiah's eyes.

"And if you don't do your part," the leader of the bunch
stated. "Every one of us will take a part off of you, hunt
down your kids, and make them eat it."

Another of the group nodded slowly. "Right before we
make them scream loud enough to wake you in your
grave."

Jeremiah didn't even try to hide the hatred in his eyes.
But rather than act on it, he choked it down and nodded
slowly. "I'm in this for the money, just like you all. And
when it's over . . . it's over."

Knowing that he was walking that terrible line once again, Jeremiah felt his heart pounding in his chest and felt the inside of his mouth suddenly turn drier than a desert floor. In the back of his mind, he could almost hear the last seconds of his life ticking away as all four gunmen silently considered the idea of killing him and taking their chances with the vault.

Finally, the leader turned away from the rest and continued walking. "Fuck him and his kids. He knows his place. Let's go."

The group walked down the street and away from the crowds, heading through a dark section of Fourth Avenue between the saloons and hotels. And just when the air was its most quiet and its most calm, it was suddenly filled with the sound of rushing footsteps and the crack of two solid objects slamming against each other.

Jeremiah's first thought was that he'd been shot and was seconds away from feeling the pain. But when he checked, there was no blood on his body. The man next to him, however, dropped to the ground as though he'd somehow fallen asleep in mid-stride.

FORTY-THREE

The first killer fell almost at Jeremiah's feet, landing with his head lying next to the fist-sized rock that had put him down. Before his body had even stopped moving, the rest of the killers had scattered and taken up positions on either side of the street.

"Who the hell did that?" the killers' leader shouted, his gun instinctively pointing toward Jeremiah.

Although Jeremiah knew he hadn't thrown anything, he was sure that the incident was more than enough of an excuse for the killers to do what they've been wanting to do since Brody forced them to watch him. He instinctually dropped to the ground and waited for the shot to come that would put him out for good.

A shot did come, but it came from the completely opposite direction than he'd been expecting. Jeremiah flinched reflexively at the loud crack that sounded through the air and heard the bullet whip over his head. But rather than strike him, the piece of lead kept going and sparked off the gun in the lead killer's hand.

"Spread out," the leader said to the two of his followers who were still on their feet. "Find where that shot came from and—"

But the rest of his orders were swallowed up when another shot barked through the night. This time, the killers were able to see the flash from the gun's muzzle, aimed their pistols in that direction and pulled their triggers.

Gunshot after gunshot blasted the peace and quiet that had been in that stretch of street only moments ago. Each time one went off, the flash it made illuminated Jeremiah's face for a fleeting second, making him cringe in expectation that one of those shots were meant for him. Although bullets were hissing in the air over his head, none of them came his way and he lifted his eyes to get a better look around.

Not a stranger to gunfire, Jeremiah quickly noticed that the only ones still doing any shooting were Brody's men. And rather than make them aware of that fact just yet, he looked around for any trace of the person who'd started the whole thing. Judging by the nature of the opening shot, Jeremiah had a fairly good idea who was behind it.

Jeremiah crawled on his belly toward the alley where the first gunshot had originated. He wasn't even halfway there when he saw something moving in a nearby shadow.

"Hey!" Jeremiah yelled while pointing toward the alley. "He's there. He's right there!"

The shots stopped for a second and when they realized the return fire was no longer coming, the killers scurried to take up positions closer to the alley.

"What did you see?" the leader asked. "Tell me or you die right now!"

But Jeremiah was already pointing to the alley, gesturing wildly when he noticed that all three guns were pointing in his direction. "Right there! Don't you see it?"

Just when the leader was about to move toward Jeremiah, one of the other killers spoke up. "He's right. I see something."

There was some movement in one of the darker shadows at the mouth of the alley. Whatever it was, it crept down low on its belly, trying to go by unnoticed.

Jeremiah waited until he knew all three killers were at their tensest moment before jumping to his feet and shouting, "Shoot him! Shoot him!"

Acting more out of reflex than anything else, the killers squeezed their trigger. Their shots tore apart the corner of one building, sending the creeping shadow into a dead run in an attempt to seek cover from the sudden storm of lead. Seeing the motion, the killers kept firing until their hammers fell upon empty cylinders.

Once the echo of gunfire rolled down the street like thunder passing overhead, the killers stepped forward while reloading their weapons.

One of the men went to the shadow, which had been stilled after getting hit by countless rounds, and nudged the thing with his boot. The shape wasn't as big as it seemed in the heat of a moment, but it was fairly large . . . for a cat.

"What the hell?" one of the killers grunted.

The leader turned around sharply, another threat prepared in his mind to unleash upon Jeremiah the moment he laid eyes on the man. But the prisoner wasn't the first man he saw. In fact, he didn't even recognize the man that had snuck up directly behind him.

"Not exactly a cat lover, huh?" Clint said to the confused gang member. And before the killer could respond, Clint slammed his fist into the man's jaw, snuffing him out like a candle with one well-placed blow.

Jeremiah wasn't at all surprised to see Clint. In fact, he'd been hoping to run into him sometime real soon. Taking advantage of the situation, he did something else that he'd been hoping to do ever since he'd been dragged away from his homestead. Balling up both fists, he buried one in the leader's stomach and then sent the other into a downward strike that clipped the other man on the side of the mouth.

The leader spat out a string of blood and saliva while bringing his gun up to bear on Jeremiah. "Warned you . . ." he said while snapping back the hammer. His finger had the trigger halfway pulled when a shot sounded from behind Jeremiah, hissing past the prisoner and digging deep into the leader's chest.

Jeremiah stepped aside, allowing Clint to move forward with his gun trained on the last remaining gang member who was still upright. Shooting him a warning look, Clint raised the Colt to sight straight down the barrel, more for effect than an actual need to take aim.

The killer barely even gave Clint much notice. Instead, he focused his attention on Jeremiah. The longer he looked at the former prisoner, the angrier he seemed to get. "You traitorous bastard," he seethed. And without missing a beat, he lifted his pistol to hip level . . . and tossed it to the ground at Clint's feet.

Nodding to Jeremiah, Clint said, "Pick it up."

Jeremiah bent at the knees, lowering himself to the pistol without taking his eyes away from the killer. He was expecting the gang member to try something when he was vulnerable. All he got was a spiteful glare. Just when his hand closed around the gun, however, Jeremiah saw the killer take in a deep breath and send a wad of spit onto his gun as well as Jeremiah's hand.

FORTY-FOUR

"Put your hands behind your back," Clint said, fighting back the urge to make the killer pay for his disgusting insult. Turning back to Jeremiah, he said, "Help me tie these fellas up and get them out of here before more of them come to check out the noise."

Taking the rope that Clint had been carrying around his shoulder, Jeremiah bound the killer's hand and feet, securing them with several knots. He knew the ropes were uncomfortable enough, but just to make sure, he tightened them just a little bit more.

Clint busied himself with the unconscious gunmen and was tying up the second one when Jeremiah came to help.

"Can you lift one over your shoulder?" Clint asked once all the killers were tightly bound.

Jeremiah reached down and effortlessly pulled a man up off the ground. "No problem."

Clint took his own load and pointed his gun at the killer who stood on his own feet. "It'll be easier for you to walk on your own," he said to the seething killer. "But not much. Drag that body out of the open and we can be on our way."

The message was understood perfectly and though the

killer let his distaste for both men show through clearly, he went where he was led and didn't put up much of a fuss. Sticking to alleys and backstreets, the strange caravan headed for the hotel where Clint was storing the other gang members when Jeremiah spoke up.

"Where are my children?" he asked. "Are they safe?"

"Yes, sir. They're tucked away safe and sound, but they sure do miss their father. If it's all the same to you, I'd rather not say any more in mixed company," Clint explained while pointing toward the killer walking in front of him.

"I understand. How can I ever thank you for what you've done?"

"A good start would be to tell me why that gang's leader went through so much trouble to get you when he had so many men of his own already."

"Brody's got plenty of men," Jeremiah said. "But not one that can crack open a bank vault like me."

Clint nodded. "I heard you were some kind of specialist."

"I can safely say I'm not bragging when I tell you I'm the best there is in this part of the country. And Brody knew if he had a chance of getting in and out of the Haddleville vault before he was cut to pieces by the guards, he needed someone who could do the job fast. I was his only hope. At least I'm the only one he's ever heard of who could do it."

"You mentioned the guards. What about the law?"

"The law hopes Brody makes it even more than he does," Jeremiah said distastefully. "They're set to get one hell of a cut for letting him work. The bank hires private guards and they're not in Brody's pocket."

"That bank must be one hell of an employer if they can keep their own guards more honest than the town law."

"They pay well enough, but they also make it known that they'll pay even more to a bounty hunter that brings in any guard who decides to work for the wrong side. The bank pays well and they only pay for bodies, not prisoners."

Clint whistled softly. "Now that's what I call an insurance policy."

They were almost at the hotel by this point and Clint steered the group around toward a back entrance. The killer at the front of the line was starting to get nervous since he recognized the fact that they were sneaking through the night, heading for a bad part of town.

Climbing up a set of rickety stairs that scaled the rear of the building and led to the room that Clint had paid extra to get, the group entered what looked to be an attic that had been converted to a medium-sized room with a ceiling that was so low, it forced every man to bend down to keep from bumping his head.

When the killer got a look at the inside of the room, his jaw nearly hit the dirty floor. "Jesus," he whispered.

Every piece of secondhand furniture that had been in the room was pushed to the sides. The bed and both chairs were lined up along one wall and several other chairs were taking up most of the rest of the room. But the furniture attracted hardly any of the killer's attention. Instead, he couldn't take his eyes off the figures that were stored in the room like so many dry goods.

There was a member of Brody's gang tied to every one of the five chairs, two lashed to the bed by ropes that had been looped around the entire frame and mattress, as well as two others who were bound so tightly that they resembled gigantic inchworms squirming on the floor. Every one of them was gagged, but still tried to shout when they saw the door open. The muffled voices filled the room with an eerie hum.

In stark contrast to the look of horror on all the gunmen's faces, Clint and Jeremiah shook their heads and smiled broadly at the sight. Jeremiah even started to laugh.

"You have been a busy man this evening," Jeremiah said as he dumped the man he'd been carrying beside the bed. "How did you do this?"

Clint put his load down and set about lashing additional ropes around all the new arrivals. "A little trap here and a little ambush there. It wasn't too hard, really. Especially since they did me the service of sticking together in groups. Some of them seemed to prefer testing my speed on the draw rather than wait here until I can send some trustworthy marshals here to pick them up."

Jeremiah's eyes widened a little further. "How many did you get in all?"

"Well, there's nine here now and these three make twelve. Plus, three of them are dead, so that makes fifteen in all."

Shoving the killer who'd walked in with them to the floor after making sure he wouldn't be able to move, Jeremiah slapped his knee and extended a congratulatory hand to Clint. "That only leaves six more of Brody's gang."

Finishing up with his prisoners, Clint double-checked the lock he'd rigged on the door and motioned for Jeremiah to follow him back out to the back staircase. "Yeah," he said, still unwilling to share in Jeremiah's enthusiasm. "But he's got to know that his men are disappearing. I can only hope that we can track them down before they skip town."

Both men descended the stairs and started heading for the alley. "They won't skip anywhere," Jeremiah said. "Not without taking a crack at that bank. Brody's too stubborn to just up and leave. And as far as knowing about his men, they were all supposed to meet at the bank for the job. Until then, even he doesn't know where they are. Hell, *they* didn't know where *he* was. Probably off fucking one of his whores, I'd expect."

Clint let out a deep breath. "That's a relief. When I saw them switch patrols and fade away, I was thinking they might be moving as separate groups. That's why I started picking them off like this and prayed they wouldn't be missed until I could round up the rest. But once he sees none of his men are there to meet him, Brody might just call off the job."

"Not if he thinks he's still got a chance of pulling it off," Jeremiah stated.

"But the only way for him to think that would be . . ."

"If I showed up like nothing was wrong."

Clint shook his head slowly at first and then sped up the longer he considered the idea. "No. I can't allow that. Once Brody knows things have gone wrong, he'll probably kill you first just out of spite. I've gone through too much trouble to get you back alive just to have you go and get yourself killed. Besides, I've got a promise to keep."

"I promised my children I'd see them again and I mean to do just that. If Brody isn't brought down now, he'll just come back to kill me and mine later, anyway. This is the only way, Clint."

"Fine," Clint said, stopping near a pile of garbage in the alley behind the hotel. "Then we'll have to make sure Brody is comfortable right up to the point when we give him a little surprise."

"Surprise?"

Kicking over a crate that had been propped against a building, Clint revealed a huge pile covered by a scrap piece of burlap. When he removed the burlap, Clint revealed all the guns he'd taken from the gang members he'd captured. "His surprise is that his prisoner will suddenly grow some teeth," Clint said while handing Jeremiah a pistol.

Jeremiah took the weapon and made sure it was loaded. Although he seemed uncomfortable with the gun, he didn't seem at all unfamiliar with it.

"Is there anything else you can tell me about the robbery?" Clint asked. "Anything you might have heard to help us close the noose on these robbers?"

"Just two small things," Jeremiah said while tucking the gun in his waistband and covering it with his shirt. "The robbery is set to happen at midnight. Also, I've got a good idea where Brody is supposed to meet up with me and the crew we just put to bed."

Clint smiled and nodded appreciatively. "You know something? We might just have a better chance of pulling this off than I'd thought."

FORTY-FIVE

Brody was feeling good. Real good. He'd gotten his information from the vice president of the First Bank of Haddleville, Sherman Pierce himself. He'd gotten his hooks into Jeremiah Garver, the best man with vaults in the country. And he'd even pulled together a gang of men who not only worked hard but followed orders. He'd told them to watch the bank and not be seen until it was time to move and so far, he hadn't seen hide nor hair of most of them for a better part of the night.

"What's the matter, Marcus?" Brody asked as they walked down Cottonwood Street. "We're all about to become very, very rich. Why the long face?"

Marcus shook his head. "Something's not right. Where are the rest of the men?"

Walking on either side of Marcus and Brody were two of their gunmen. Brody waited until they got in sight of the bank and searched the darkness for the shapes he knew should be there. At first, he didn't see much of anything. But after a few more seconds ticked by, he picked out a set of shadows lurking in a nearby alley. "There's three of them over there," he said.

"I already seen them," Marcus replied. "I'm talking

about the rest. I've been looking in the posts we picked out for them and haven't seen any more but them three. By my count, we're short at least ten men."

Brody stopped in his tracks. His eyes narrowed and he held his breath while peering into the night. "You're right. And where's Jeremiah? He and the others should have been here by—"

Brody's question was cut off when he heard footsteps approaching from behind. Both he and Marcus spun around and drew their guns when they spotted a familiar face.

"Don't shoot," Jeremiah whispered. "It's just me."

"Where're the others who were with you?" Marcus asked. "What happened to everyone?" Without waiting for an answer, he turned to Brody and said, "This is no good. Something's going on here and I say we get the hell out of here right now."

The other men with Brody were shifting nervously on their feet. They'd pulled their guns as well and were turning from side to side, looking for a target.

Every thought running through Brody's mind was so strong, it might as well have been shouted out at the top of his lungs. He glared at the empty streets around the bank, the guards still walking on patrol, over to Jeremiah and Marcus, and then finally back to the bank. Suddenly, reaching over to grab hold of Jeremiah by the arm, Brody snapped the hammer of his pistol back and started moving toward the bank.

The guards had just walked around the corner of the building, so he made sure to keep his steps quick. "To hell with this. I ain't getting a better shot at this place than right now."

Marcus started to protest, but before he could get a word out, gunfire erupted from somewhere in the surrounding shadows. None of the bullets came at Brody or any of his men. Instead, they sparked against the side of the bank, tearing pieces away from the building where the guards had just been.

The sound brought the guards running back and they were just in time to see the trio of gunmen who had been waiting in the alley come out from hiding to head for Brody's side. There were more gunshots fired from the darkness, which was more than enough to put the already nervous guards over the edge.

None of the three gang members even saw the guards had returned and were too busy running toward Brody with their guns out and at the ready. The moment they caught sight of the guards running toward them, they took aim at the bank's shooters, but didn't get to pull their triggers before the guards opened fire.

All three of the gunmen were cut down in a hail of blazing lead before they made it so far as the bank's front door.

Marcus pulled his trigger and dropped one of the guards. He was just about to pick off another when he heard a voice coming from behind him.

"I wouldn't," Clint said.

Hearing that, Marcus and one of the remaining gunmen who'd been trailing behind Brody spun around to face the man who'd just spoken.

"Who the hell are you?" Marcus asked.

"Either the man who puts you in jail, or the one who puts you in the ground. Take your pick."

Marcus looked over to the man beside him and they both made their choice together. After a subtle nod, Marcus brought his gun up to bear on Clint, knowing that the man at his side would do the same.

Drawing the Colt and aiming with a motion so quick that it almost couldn't be seen, Clint squeezed off a round that drilled through Marcus' side and spun the man around like a top. Without pausing, he shifted his aim to the second man and sent another round through that one's chest before either of the others could take a shot.

The gunman next to Marcus fell flat on his face, but Marcus himself was fighting to stay on his feet. He glared at Clint and sucked in a breath though clenched teeth while bringing his arm up so he could aim.

Clint let the killer have another second to make his choice but when he saw the look in Marcus's eyes, he knew that choice had already been made. The Colt bucked once more in Clint's hand, sending another round through the air that sprayed Marcus's brains behind him.

Before Marcus's body hit the dirt, Clint was running over to Brody and Jeremiah. As far as he could tell, there was still one more guard left standing and another on one knee, clutching a messy wound in his stomach.

"Brody!" Clint yelled.

The distraction was enough to draw the attention of the gunman standing next to Brody just long enough for him to take his eyes away from the bank guards. The guard who was kneeling lifted his rifle to his shoulder and sent a bullet into the back of the gunman's head, leaving Brody standing alone with Jeremiah still in tow.

"Hold it!" Clint yelled to the guards. "He's got a hostage!"

The guards had seen Clint take out some of the robbers and listened to what he had to say. They lowered their weapons, but were ready to use them at a moment's notice.

"Yeah," Brody said, sensing his advantage. "And me and this here hostage are going to walk out of here. Ain't that right, Jeremiah?" When Brody glanced at his prisoner, he didn't see a man who would do or say anything to remain in his favor. What he saw was a man full of rage. A man who had been pushed too far. A man holding a gun in his face.

"Think about your kids, Jeremiah," Brody hissed.

"Believe me," Jeremiah replied steadily. "I am." And with that, he pulled the trigger.

The smoke was still thick in the air when Clint walked over to Jeremiah's side. They were soon joined by the two guards who hobbled over to look down at the men bleeding at their feet. Although both guards had been hit, they both seemed to be moving around well enough. Even the man Clint thought was dead seemed to be propping himself up against the building.

"Jesus Christ," the guard with the rifle said. "That's Brody Saunders! There's one hell of a reward on that one's head . . . along with most of these others."

Confirming the observation with a nod, the other guard took Clint's and Jeremiah's hands, shaking them vigorously. "You two are rich men. Not to mention that we owe you our lives."

Since Jeremiah was in shock, Clint spoke up on his behalf. "I'd say we're even in that last respect. If you hadn't come running when you did . . ."

"Just doing our jobs. Come back in the mornin'. Mr. Pierce will want to hand you your rewards personally."

"I think I can handle that job after I send word for the U.S. Marshals to come pick up some trash I collected. And until then," Clint said, slapping Jeremiah on the back, "My friend here's got some family to visit."

Jeremiah stared at Clint with a dazed look in his eyes. "Clint . . . I . . . I don't have the words. How can I ever repay you?"

"Oh, I don't know. How's ten percent of that reward sound?"

Watch for

THE DOOMSDAY RIDERS

250th novel in the exciting GUNSMITH series
from Jove

Coming in October!